PURE
SLUSH
BOOKS

hapPy²

pure slush
vol. 15

First published as a collection January 2018

Pure Slush Books
32 Meredith Street
Sefton Park SA 5083
Australia

Email: edpureslush@live.com.au
Website: http://pureslush.webs.com
Store: http://pureslush.webs.com/store.htm

Original cover photograph by Janiece Pope
Cover design by Matt Potter

ISBN: 978-1-925536-39-3

Also available as an eBook
ISBN: 978-1-925536-40-9

A note on differences in punctuation and spelling

Pure Slush Books proudly features writers from all over the English-speaking world. Some speak and write English as their first language, while for others, it's their second or third or even fourth language. Naturally, across all versions of English, there are differences in punctuation and spelling, and even in meaning. These differences are reflected in the work *Pure Slush Books* publishes, and accounts for any differences in punctuation, spelling and meaning found within these pages.

Contents

Poetry

Poetry

Dye works

Bridget Kursheed

Twelve thousand murex shells that summer in Naples
to check Friedlander's chemical indigo
against royal purple. It did not match
its clotted blood. He made that too. And sold it.

Think about Capri and blues; that bit of sea
where Neapolitans cling together
in the boat's bottom, each rowing bench
as hard by as their own warm ribs.

And the cameos a slate-blue in paper boxes
on stalls amongst the Roman gravestones.
The puff of ochre smoke as couples stop
in the bothy of volcanic fumes for health.

Or lemons. Or watermelons selling to tourists.
Black sand and paid for royal blue deckchairs.
And skin as brown as boys diving for pennies
happy, the shine of water on them, holiday colour.

Ripples

Claudia Bierschenk

Pain pushes me
out of bed at midnight.

I count the minutes,
Up and down the room,
A concrete balloon
Inflating, deflating inside me.

I call the midwife at three am,
feel guilty for getting her
Out of bed, regardless of the
fact that she's the one
with me in this,
And shouldn't I feel happy now?

She can tell over the phone,
This will take time,
So I watch "the three amigos"
Between seismic ripples in my body.

Twelve hours later,
I am stranded
on a complicated bed,
and wonder
If I'll be alive by the end of this.

Someone says
"Don't hold her neck like that."
And between drug-induced delight,
Tiredness, and murderous pain,
Your small body,
wet with my blood.

Ah, there you are.

Love in the
Little Shop of Happiness

Allan J. Wills

We come to town for coffee, cake, and milkshakes in the bistro,
then stroll under the verandas, window shopping. My children
sense your shop is a sanctuary, with its playpen, books for all
ages, quirky homewares and casual fashions. They lead me to
it.

And then there is you,
    with your raven hair and smile.
    Like the covers of a novel
    our faces
    conceal their stories yet beguile.

In another world,
    at another time, we might
    be lovers in some romantic tale.
    Small gestures a précis
    of imagined drama danced so light.

I am content in the sanctuary of your little shop too. So the
children and I tarry a while and buy a card or a book some-
times, before strolling on and returning home to our true love.

The Professor and the Eggplant

Thomas M. McDade

Unlike the first semester chump who acted as if we were enrolled
in pre-med, this professor was a reasonable man, a regular guy,
undemanding and very rarely boring, always happy and smiling.
A Connecticut wildflower maven, a book he wrote did well in
bookstore chains and likewise in mom and pop concerns.
The only lecture I recall embraced the eggplant.
All that remains in mind, specifically, other than his love
for that shiner of a vegetable—all-time favorite
in his home garden, was his regret that no nutritional worth
was to be found in that ovoid.
No student ever raised a hand to speak of the indigo
star and pinwheel appeal of that veggie's blossom
to score points.
A heart attack killed this good man young and I
reasoned his favorite dish was not baba ganoush
rather deep fried rounds hidden under Parmesan
that clung to his arterial walls like students
glomming onto courses professors with gentle
reputations taught.

China Cup

Lucy Tyrrell

Another *happy birthday* courses past in fleeing lope.
Even threadbare memories caught in translucent amber
fail
to hold this day
more
lovingly than delicate china cup holds hot green tea.
I mustn't squander weeping on
slipped-time yesterdays.

happy pappy sappy crappy

Ruth Sabath Rosenthal

undone…gone…swansong…belongings…*A Longing to be happy!*

out…shout…bout…blackout…take-out…*Out stain out!*

old…bold…cold…sold…told…retold…resold…*Behold, a Pale Horse!*

unwell…inkwell…swell…pell-mell…*For Whom the Bell Tolls.*

all…ball…call…stall…stool pigeon…evil…*All's Well that Ends Well?*

gray…day…haze…heyday…wayward…A-OK…*Hey Diddle Diddle.*

fill…will…ill…illness…willy-nilly…willpower…*Power to the people!*

birthright…girth…tight…heights…mighty…*May the righteous prevail!*

goodnight…deadwood…hoodlum…goodbye…knighthood…*God is good!*

words…worth…Wordsworth…birdwatcher…*Killing Him Softly with Words.*

poetic…poetry…try…tree…triage…tic-toc…tic-tac-toe…*Trial by Jury.*

trail…travail…ail…flail…bale…fail…*Wailing the Jailbird Blues!*

A Stitch in Time

Jan Chronister

No one sews anymore
except daughters in sweatshops
with covered windows
breathing dust-filled air
sore fingers running
machines that clang away all day

Students puzzle over labels
naming places their parents
can't locate, countries where
shirtless children wear shadows
of empty stomachs
crowded beds.

Women walk out of department store sales
happy with how much they saved.

Apples

Em König

Apples leave
A crunching sound nestled
In gums

Gargling over
Every time patience
Is lost

The flicks of coloured skin
And white flesh
Rot

With a smile
Through the teeth you can smell
Its age

Make a Wish

Kindra McDonald

imagined the future
as an art deco Metropolis,
all shine and chrome
sleek and scalloped—

"The Jetsons" meets "The Jeffersons."
There would be teleportation,
telekinesis, pneumatic tubes for travel,
and my family would always be together.

I thought we would all be living on Mars
by now, communicating with so many
different civilizations we had all learned
Esperanto and discoveries occurred so

many times per day, there were whole
cities devoted to cataloging new species.
Flowers that changed color based
on who looked at them, the fish that

competed to hold their breath the longest
on land, and the detailed study of Mars birds would
allow us to recreate flight, as we preened our feathers
and understood inherently our wild purpose

yet every year on August 5th, the Curiosity Rover sings
"Happy Birthday" to itself, the universal tune echoing
lonely through the cold dark vast.

Dear Half Tablet
of Valium

Susan Doble Kaluza

again you've
saved me from what I'd
otherwise conjecture
is 18th century dentistry.
I'm especially appreciative
of your smooth limousine ride
out of the wilderness
of pain, or the fear of it
which is not fear itself,
but some fear facsimile
in the form of needles
and wheelie things that bite
and buzz and bruise. Sorry
I couldn't devour the whole
of you, you happy, sun-yellow
surprise, offering ouch-less levels
of blissful security far above my
Pac Man mentality for prescription
abuse. But while in the waiting area
where they keep patients in what
I once heard referred to as *suspended zulu*

sequestered in bucket chairs that closely
resemble those of a Volkswagen Beetle
and perhaps several years' subscriptions
to both Needle Point and National
Geographic, I snapped you in two
without the use of a knife or my teeth and with
all the self-control of tearing into a bag of Lays.
Hence, you're a bit ragged in appearance,
but nonetheless processing things like
an entire vat of Oregon grapes fermenting
and simmering inside
my veins. The problem is
I'm on a deadline to which
there is less than a day attached
to a reading fee, for which I desire
to not repeat *to or for which*, but
to free my thinking without
clouding my vision or short
circuiting my brain [which] is,
just now, functioning barely
above sea level, more in the mode of
something blinking on and off like the light
on my PC with its Windows Vista software
struggling to read my printer. But
ever so much thank you
for your gentle hand, O Valium
truly you're up in there
like sex and vodka, maybe one of those
swim up bars attended by men in long
dreadlocks talking   really   slow
and smiling wide like whoever
those native peoples are in the magazines
who bear their teeth and gums
and swallow the sun whole.

17

Mokopuna

Nod Ghosh

The muslin of your skin,
the hollow of your bones
the shadow of your temples
the glory of your cry
the curl of your fingers
around my age-worn touch

the gesture of your arm-swing
the mint-kiss of your breath
all these I have loved
and will carry with me
in the folds of my being

your glacier eyes
the complication of your ears
all these and more
will stay with me
when we are apart

live well
young one.

Good Wishes

Kersten Christianson

May dogs always wander
the rooms of your heart.

May you wake to raucous wind
and waves wherever you sleep.

May the shelved chapbooks beckon
in whispered voices to sit and read.

May stillness provide you serenity;
sweet escape.

May letters from friends
fill your mailbox.

May the gathered blank books
fill their pages with words.

Moving In

Robert Beveridge

your bar of soap
rests on the side
of the tub

wet towel
hangs on the rack

fills me
with comfort

Happy Hour

Colin W. Campbell

A good time for another new bottle,
so graceful, discerning and mindful.
What's just ahead
is an empty head,
as the world goes round, in a wobble.

Happy Accidents

John Lambremont Sr.

If we hadn't promised Sarah
to cat-sit her cat at our house,
I wouldn't have been sent out
to the dollar general store
for a cat-scratch mat.

If I hadn't been sent out
to the dollar general store,
I would not have found
the Daniel Lanois CD
at the thrift store next door.

If the Mardi Gras website
had not contained an error,
we would have never gone to Madisonville
for a boat float parade
that had launched the week before.

If my wife hadn't had to pee,
we wouldn't have gone to Morton's
in Madisonville for the first time
for some of the best fried seafood
I have ever had anywhere.

If we had not gone to Madisonville,
we wouldn't have taken a slow ride
across the Northshore countryside
along old Highway 22
all the way to Slidell.

If the sign hadn't said
Business Route U.S. 190,
I wouldn't have turned back
to find downtown Slidell,
but would have gone straight on
into Mississippi.

If I hadn't trusted the railroad tracks,
I wouldn't have turned left at them,
and would have missed completely
what was once downtown Slidell;
they call it Old Town now.

If we hadn't gone into Old Town,
we would not have found
the silver fox fur stole
at the antique mall; my wife
said don't tell Sarah, as she
doesn't approve of furs,
but I think I just
did.

If we hadn't gone in the antique mall,
we wouldn't have seen the old sweet shop
just up the street and around the corner
that featured hand-made ice cream;
we had chocolate coconut
and creole cream cheese.

If Daniel's instrumental album
hadn't been so ambient and radiant,
I wouldn't have been so relaxed:
I didn't get a speeding ticket
in St. Tammany Parish
this time.

Another Morning

Judah Eli Cricelli

Let it send
A silent friend,
Eat my mind from inside-end,
Buzz with me, I'll be a bee,
Stutter
Swallow
Half of me.
Headache morning,
Movement where? A
Strand of hair that's
Over there, a phospholipid
Coil coil
Drawn-out stare
And stop me there
I'll stop me there,
I pick
My skin
Beyond
Repair,
Alive and well,
And mostly fine,
I'm just un-happy by design.

Too Much Happiness

Rick Blum

Happiness
a tiresome spouse
always a smile
not one to grouse

Wakes each morn
to chirping of birds
Ends every eve
with comforting words

Never sad
she floats through the day
inside a cloud
of silver inlay

Joy she spreads
devoid of fatigue
Gotta admit
she's out of my league

So I must
cut to the chase
though I try hard
I just can't keep pace

Happiness
with you I am done
now let's go out
and have us some fun

Norwich Terrier Explains How to Dig a Hole

Lisa Stice

begin with purpose
an end-goal to unearth
a secret: a bumble bee
sleeping underground
or a squirrel's hoard
or a root that winds
its way and begs you
to keep tossing dirt
until a small hill grows
behind you, then lie down
and rest in the coolness
of your creation

Saturation

John Herold

Walking naked I soak
in warm rain,
greenness of life, and
sensation of moss
under happy feet.

I grin, lost
in the patter of raindrops hitting broad leaves,
in feeling trickles of water along my curves,
and I almost think
of going back for my clothing.

Long beat

Piet Nieuwland

Air here is salt sweet fresh, warm,
Surf crisp, clean just gone low water
Night king tide wash left
Tuatua, whelk messages
From cloud balconies
A precursor squall looms
For the next tropical wet mass
But for now, it's just hoof prints
Red beaked gull and tern couplets, wings
Quiet as hallucinations
There is little more to do, remove shirts,
Make a plunge green glisten let scented foam
Take away tension
Turn and let wave
Spill, carry us,
Carry us, carry us back
To a dark chocolate fig snack
Watch massed pingao pulse with white horses
A sloop emerges, in this wind, it could be
A skiddingly fast fun slide
To a Whangaparapara sheltered
Anchorage with kaka, not rua-kaka
More like poly-kaka, for that's how it is here
With space enough
To breathe and bend
Happy at the dunes, Friday, late April

Moon

Shane Guthrie

On our last night the moon was full
The sky was uncharacteristically clear

It was dangerous crossing the bridge home
The silver on the water was so beautiful

Of course, I didn't know it was the last night
And in the morning I was looking forward to more of you

In the afternoon of our last day I was full of hope
But it was no big surprise, I'd expected it from the first day

It was actually one of the best times to end

The sun cut through the clouds and I only needed a t-shirt
To be warm and happy in the world

I can't decide

Sunayna Pal

I can't decide on what's more endearing,
A butterfly
Or a child seeing one fly for the first time.

I can't decide on what's more cute,
A child trying to save a drop of yogurt
Or that he ends up spilling the whole cup.

I can't decide who is more satisfied,
The child who eats on his own
Or the mother who watches him do so.

I can't decide who is more excited,
The child throwing the ball for the first time
Or the mother who spent days teaching this to him.

I can't decide who the teacher is,
The mother
Or the child.

i have been patient

Leigh Marques

i have sat and watched petals
unfold, dew dry up
in the morning, shadows
toss colors around. i have
brought myself here
to this moment and
i have felt pride.

No Tests

Judy Shepps Battle

My practice
is to be present

to breathe in the moment
to feel it ride inner current

hew a path to ancient pain
swaddle, coo, and

heal before being
exhaled as a love offering

before joining with other
nanoseconds to form time,

shape history, and create
biography.

My practice
dissolves perception

reveals patterns and colors
gasps at raw beauty

no need to describe
no need to remember

no tests!

only permission to be simple
to observe, feel, and release

the inviolable *what is*
and be happy.

A Question of Partnership

Alex Robertson

Appreciation for one's lot
But to the extent of Sodom and Gomorrah?
A biblical interpretation of heaven and hell
Realised in real life
Pure Imagination as Willy Wonka sings
    revealing realities
Each book or story a "how to guide"
Mostly on how to live a merry existence
Keeping a positive approach
In crowds or solitude
    and for those requiring to
    keep the Black Dog at bay

Different definitions of what happy is…
Organisms and orgasms
For the purpose of supplication of life
With sentient beings looking for pleasure
Raw flesh or fantasy
    depending on one's taste
Animals doing what they only know
Humans able to communicate whims
    thoughts of past to future
Mindfulness keeping us in the moment

Marriage seen as a consummation of joy
Regardless of gender
A decision to commit
    declarations of intent
Official recognition the meaning of contentment
If only the politicians would follow
Jean-Luc Picard's directive
    and "Make it so!"

Palate Cleanser

Martin Jon Porter

driving home from work –

friday afternoon rain
Flushing the week away

Ο Στρυμόνας

(The Strymonas)

Margarita Serafimova

The cows were swimming,
the cows were headed to the other bank.
The light was dancing for them.

Mexico Happy

John Grey

I long to live at this speed but my
blood won't have it.
If only I could sit outside my hacienda
sipping tequila with friends.
with sombreros swamping our heads,
so wide they make day night.

I long to nap but I'm wide awake here.
The heat stills the cactus
but its wind blows me along.
I don't have it in me
to knead tortilla flour, mix spices,
to strum a guitar for a senorita
in a candle-lit window.

And I can't join the funeral parades,
everyone in masks, blowing, clanging noise-makers,
so loud, so joyous, surely nobody can be dead.
All this happiness, they almost make me
believe there really is a better place.
But I can't help thinking it's just the weather
and it's not my weather.
It's the weather in their heads,
dry and dusty but when it finally does rain,
it's overgrown with wild chrysanthemums,
with roses like the people
come back out of the earth.

I'm Northern. I'm white.
The sum of all my sensibilities is their refusal
to let me go.
I don't see the beauty in purposelessness.
I don't get the happiness in sorrow.

Someone hands me a guitar in a roadside bar
and I play something weary.
People come to the window
to see that it's me,
to know they're not suddenly
from some other place.

Surf's Up

Martin Christmas

The sun is barely over the horizon
and the slight breeze adds to the chill
of a mid-January summer morning
but already the surfers arrive.

They come in their varied transports,
their small yellow V Dubs, Fords,
Mazdas and ample four wheeled drives,
all here for a dip with God.

The swell is swell and lazy,
as it crawls across the great expanse
of blue ocean, seemingly effortless
and unseating even the most confident rider.

Men and women, wet suited and
wet haired, swimming through the waves
to ride their way to Happy Heaven.
Two paddlers glide across the luscious waves
as they make their way to Nirvana.

The rising sun sharp cuts through
the surf, revealing jellyfish shapes
of uplifted sand drift that make each wave
explode with starburst patterns.
And they still ride the surf.

On shore, the once-were-surfers
stand on the beach-side cliff face dreaming
who knows what as they return their minds
to Midge Farrelly or Nat Young and themselves,
pushing through the surf of years ago.

The sun now risen over this Kingdom,
but the vehicles keep coming.
The old surfers keep dreaming,
peering, seeing long gone waves mingling
with this never ending surf.
Time ticks by and boards fly.

The pilgrimage continues.
Its devotees kneeling, squatting, squinting
in the heat of the day now.

While there's surf, there's life.

Pickup Truck

JP Lundstrom

He didn't have a lot of money
He didn't have a hundred bucks,
He wasn't that good-looking, didn't do any cooking,
But he had a pickup truck.

He never took me out to dinner
Was always way down on his luck,
He wasn't all that handy, never brought me candy,
But man! That boy could—

    Set off fireworks
    Cause shooting stars,
    Put fire in the moonlight,
    Send me to Mars.

I wouldn't call him all that brainy,
I wouldn't call him no dumb cluck,
I wouldn't hurt his pride if I wanted a ride
In that awesome pickup truck!

He had a sweetness all about him;
He had a purity of soul.
He was good to the core and a little bit more,
He had the gift of rock and—

Setting off fireworks
Shooting down stars,
Firing up the moonlight,
Sending me to Mars.

He wasn't more than I could handle.
He wasn't lightning that had struck.
He said he felt the same; I let him change my name,
We honeymooned in that old truck!

We got ourselves a little place now:
A couple chickens, and some ducks,
We got some cows, of course, and a big ol' horse,
And all we do at night is—

Set off fireworks
Cause shooting stars,
Put fire in the moonlight,
Fly back and forth to Mars.

Near Happy Valley

Don Kingfisher Campbell

You can be born at the Good Samaritan
Preschool with Little Sunshine
Attend Valentine Elementary
Go to Independence High
Graduate Golden Gate University

While living in the Jamboree Apartments
Buy a Homecoming at The Preserve home

Shop the Sunshine Convenience Market
Acquire tools through the Sunshine Supply Co., Inc.
Play on windy days thanks to the Sunshine Kite Company
I believe Sunshine Plastics can make just about anything you need
Sorry, Sunshine Clothing is no longer open

Golden Top Battery will keep your car running
Cook, because Golden Flavor Trading Inc. exists
Recreate the Golden Saddle Cyclery way
More fun can be found at the Golden Golf Mart
Satisfy your aesthetic desires via the Gold Bug Art Gallery
Sick of everything, try the Golden Elite Pharmacy

But the most happy places are happy
Happy Bakery
Happy Balloons
Happy Dollar Store (now closed due to inflation or gentrification)
Happy Donut
Happy Dragon
Happy Family Restaurant
Happy Harbor Seafood Restaurant
Happy Pet
And best of all
The Happy Ending Bar

For a real singing adventure
Either Energy Karaoke
Or Carnival Karaoke

Exhausted?
Time for Golden Road Assisted Living

Before you're dead
Choose an afterlife location
Garden's Edge for your pet
And for you, Rose Hills
Resurrection Cemetery
Hollywood Forever

Happy Birthday to Me

Mark Hudson

On November 12, 2017 I turned 47 years
old, and I woke up feeling my age. I woke up and
it was pouring rain outside. I didn't want to get
out of bed. But it was my birthday, and I had
to get up and celebrate!
　　I was worried I'd have to actually
celebrate my birthday alone. I'd even hinted
to my best friend Chris that it was my birthday,
and I was wondering if he could help me celebrate.
At the last minute he came through, picked
me up in his car, and took me out for deep-dish
pizza! I'm lucky to have friends like him!
　　A week later, my sister, accompanied by
my great niece and nephew, took me out for
Chinese food, and at first, I sat down with my
niece and nephew, and they were staring down
into their hand-held electronic devices, which
I didn't like. But eventually they began to talk.
I even had the pleasure of hearing my niece,
a fifth grade honor roll student, recite the
Gettysburg Address from pure memory.
And what really warmed my heart was
when my sister dropped me off at the train,
my niece pulled out of her pocket a hand-made

48

birthday card with a drawing of a silly girl.
It was a pleasant surprise. And my sister
had put together a photo album, with tons
of happy memories, including those of
relatives who have passed away. Through
these photos, the people live in my mind.

Then, if that were not enough, a
friend from church offered to take me
out to dinner to celebrate my birthday.
We went to a restaurant called the
Lucky Platter, which is one block from
my house, which is known for its
unique food, and paintings on the
wall that look like they were collected
from a yard sale.

They had a new sandwich that
I thought I'd try out; a brat burger
on a pretzel bun, and I ate nothing all
day to save my appetite for the meal.
Then to top it all off, my friend gave
me an additional forty dollars!

Now it is December, the
month of Christmas, the month
of giving. There is a call to be
generous. Where I live it is
really freezing. But when I go out,
people are in the holiday spirit.
So when it comes to the holidays,
I need to remember to give back
and be generous – just like people
were generous and loving to me
on my birthday!

Bath

Edward Reilly

Naked, happy in my hot bath,
The soapy water cascading over
And threatening to make a mess.
Do I care? A nip of whiskey
Helps dull the pain of losing her,
And then all the other hers
Who have drifted past my fishing net.
I have a CD of Geniušas playing,
Chopin again: I like his style,
Though it could be said he's more Russian
Than Franco-Polish, or whatever,
For there's a hard edge to the wires:
But then, I think Romanticism
Is greatly misunderstood,
By the rain-sodden English especially,
Who have forgotten the bayonets
And cannonades of Revolution,
The great disorders of peoples
Only ever hinted at in Austen,
And teachers conveniently forget
The Brontës were really Irish.
You have two left thumbs – she said,
And scales fell off the keyboard.

Whenever I descended from C,
The wooden ruler had an edge of steel.
She wasn't particularly cruel,
But harsh enough to stop my dreams
From careening into total disgrace.
I was a good-enough page-turner,
Sang in key, learnt my Latin,
Still with me like a bedside missal,
But my fingers ache at this, still.
If the mirror is less than kind,
It is just as well, lest pride swell
Me in unjustified measures,
A caution against sloppy shaving.
I'm not sure who told me this,
That the skin cannot bear too much
Sunlight, for we burn, or cold
For we would freeze to our deaths
Whether this is true, I don't know.
That irritates my sense of being,
Since the truth of all things
Is what I do in Mathematics,
As I may try to do in all other things,
Yet, to be bare as a baby, like this,
Is not an offence against God,
Nor even against Nature, we're born so,
And so will go into the gaseous berth
If I cannot pay for a slice of earth.

Of Love and Loneliness

Cynthia Leslie-Bole

one
little brown bat
(common name),
also known as
Myotis lucifugus
(scientific name),
who is one inch long,
furred in taupe suede,
and sporting round ears
of fragile leather,
nests under my deck

I first spied the scat
of this flittermouse
(Old English name)
on the colorful kayak
directly beneath
where he cozies up
between joists
during the day

upon first viewing,
inexplicably
but inexorably,
he became to me
Bernie Sanders
(given name),
although perhaps
he should have been
My Otis
(punning name),
and I loved him
as a mother loves
any small, soft creature

my joy
however
was tempered
with concern
that first summer
because one bat
does not a colony make
and loneliness
seemed to cloak Bernie
in further shadow
as he slept solo
under the deck

but the next summer
—glad tidings—
there were two:
Bernie and Bernadette
(or perhaps Bernie and Bernardo),
and I sighed contentedly
knowing my small friend
had found another
of his ilk

this summer
though
the pile of droppings
decorating the kayak
has diminished by half
and now Bernie is again
hanging alone
by his tiny toes
while I fret about
white-nose fungus
that may extirpate
(oh evil word)
all little brown bats
within
twelve years

Wikipedia says the
lifespan
of
Myotis lucifugus
is often well beyond
ten years
so now I have to worry
that Bernie may live
long enough
to be the last
little brown bat
in the world
hanging all by himself
beneath my deck
while
a little brown bit
of me
pines away
to nothing
as well

Happy Birthday

Carl 'Papa' Palmer

Sitting with bubba in his truck
waiting for the rain to slow

sharing our last can of beer
from the case we bought

with the near empty **KFC** bucket
for my daughter's birthday party.

Old Bob wagging happily
after seeing us pull up

dances on the front porch
howls his hound dog howl

brings both wives out the door
to stand and stare with Bob.

Neither appear to be as loving
as when we left six hours ago

for our quick trip to the store
leaving them to greet the guests.

Prose

Prose

Winner

Irene Buckler

On pension day, the gaming room is full. Seniors unable to resist the siren call of the poker machines arrive early for their fortnightly flutter and take up residence in front of their favourite machines.

Tom acknowledges Mrs O'Leary and Mr Wong as they play. As usual, she's chasing her pot of gold on the Wild Leprechaun machine and he's pinning his hopes for good fortune on the Emperor Dragon machine. Tom doesn't have a favourite machine. He knows that all poker machines, even the Irish and Chinese themed ones preferred by Mrs O'Leary and Mr Wong, pay at the same rate as all the others.

Nobody's talking except the machines and they're going off all over the place with upbeat jingles and happy noises that Tom would find irritating in any other setting. In here, though, where day can pass unseen into night under subdued artificial lighting, he associates the electronic sound effects with money. In fact, everywhere Tom looks, he sees money. He's certain that nobody, including dear old Mrs O'Leary or Mr Wong, will be striking it rich today under the hypnotic spell of this place, but he's not like anyone else in the gaming room. As the pulsating poker machines slowly eat away their money, everyone's losing, but not Tom. He has it all worked out and he never loses because he owns the joint.

Happy Enough

Len Kuntz

You took my pulse and told me, "If it was any lower you'd be dead."

We sat in the waiting area, just us, ignoring the milk-colored marble floor tiles and the mahogany walls.

You said, "Dead men tell no tales," and winked, with a mint julep sparkle in your celadon eyes, so sassy and sure.

You opened a can somehow, with what I don't know, plopping out olives, sticking them on the ends of your fingertips before biting them off with your mouth and chewing. Instead of swallowing, you stretched out your jaw, revealing a disgusting mush of slime while pointing at the mess with both forefingers in some kind of epileptic gang member sign.

"What?" I asked.

"See food," you gurgled, saliva streaking down your cheek. "Get it? See food?"

I laughed a little because it was so dumb, because you were so silly and trying so hard.

You said, "Let's try this for as long as we can, see if we go blind or not," and crossed your eyes which made you appear scary, then, after a while, just a little nuts.

You said, "You're gonna have to work harder if you're gonna make it."

You said, "Some of the best games are the ones you don't buy at the store," and curled your forefinger over the side of your thumb in the shape of a mouth and said, "Gabba gabba, hey! Let's have some fun today! Whaddaya think?"

You were a stage show. Puppet master. Ventriloquist. An odd anagram, but the very distraction I needed.

In those minutes and hours, you taught me how to snap my fingers, how to curl my tongue, make my earlobe twitch. You taught me how to whistle. You told me puberty was untrustworthy, but, "Do some research beforehand. Get it?"

I didn't.

After so long, you looked at the courtroom door and then I did, too, and when my eyes grew misty you gave my thigh a sharp pinch but winked again.

"Motherfucker, toughen up," you said.

I'd never heard that word. It felt like a bolt, like some kind of freedom.

"It's important," you said. "Really, I'm even not even fucking kidding."

You told me, "I bet he picks you and she picks me, but we'll still see each other on holidays."

You said, "Lots of kids have divorced parents, but most of them seem happy enough."

When the door finally opened, you grabbed my hand and squeezed it, saying, "Go on now. Smile wide. Now's the time, if ever there was one."

And because you were my big sister, and because you were my best friend, I did what you wanted.

I sat bolt upright, at attention, and I smiled like I never had.

Black Cloud

L. Noelle McLaughlin

"The pineal gland is stimulated by both the light and the dark."

When you put the black cloud in my mouth, I make sure not to swallow, blow it out super slow and back into your ear when you look to the left for a sec.

That means I have to hold it in, so some of it seeps in through the roof of my mouth, and my brain starts to crackle too fast, and also the back of my throat wants to suck in the fire, and also the back of my front teeth and dog teeth spark and want to bite up your floppy white face, the way it reds so easy, easy breezy, then drain out like Casper come home.

You say something cozy, like you want to stuff me into a trash bag full of bootie slippers, the ones with fur inside that was only make believe, and I want to sleep even lower then breathe, but you already fed me the black cloud so I know you were only pretending to die, but you felt fine inside, and now I am going to have to put the black cloud back where it belongs.

I always seep it out sideways, so there's no doubt how it'll turn out. You get nice when you're nervous, you play the way everyone would want you to, you chew down your big nail so far so you can pretend that nobody sees it.

I believe it, the way the dark makes the animals start; I'm not one to pretend that electric lights are real. I feel

Your pulse when it slows down

The under of arches skimming the ground

The air gets shiny right before it snows.

My eye black grows when it's time to let the light in. Lick your lips and laugh a little lower; I am never over.

I read between the leaky lines, let rain soak up the happy pines.

I tongue a little taste of fate, then make us both a piled up plate.

Scales

KR Rosman

The summer I was twelve, my piano teacher's husband was busted for selling pot. I knew about it because I read his name in the newspaper round-up of drunk drivers, thieves, and drug dealers. She had a Polish name: Wachowski, narcotics distribution. She taught me songs that sounded like fairy-tales. I played only the right hand because the bass notes ruined the lightness of the songs.

Dad fired her. Watching him talk was like reading Wachowski in the newspaper all over again. His red face was the comma after Wachowski, and his hands were the semicolon separating Mr. Wachowski from the next crime. We were in the living room, in front of the piano. I pressed middle C and it felt like the room tilted a little. She cussed him a blue streak and called me a brat.

"How will I feed my kids?"

"Not my problem."

I was proud of Dad because we had problems, too. Last night Mom boiled the last of our backyard steer—the brain—then chopped-chopped-chopped-chopped it in a skillet. She gagged and cried at her own childhood, then we ate it.

"Some people," Mom said. She was in the kitchen, clattering a frozen casserole on the counter.

My dad and Mrs. Wachowski stood at the piano in the living room, and I was between them, holding my music book.

Last week Mrs. Wachowski circled the bass clef and the flats. Now she flipped her hair back and looked at me. She had my mom's wrinkles at her mouth. I hadn't known about her kids. Dad rubbed his hand over his eyes and Mom repeated herself.

"So-me people."

I didn't take Mrs. Wachowski's hand but I wanted to.

"See ya around, 'kay?" she said.

"'Kay."

She smoothed her skirt.

"I'll be fine—happy, even," she said, and left us for that bright day.

No need to worry!

Matthew Harrison

Siu-ming had been accepted for a Chemistry Masters in London, but he really didn't want to go. Another year of Chemistry was bad enough, but on top of that you had the English weather, and the food as well! How could you survive for a year on fish and chips? Yet his mother had booked the plane tickets, and Number One uncle – the patriarch now that Grandfather had passed away – had gathered his other uncles and aunties for a dim sum lunch to see him off.

"The food there isn't really that bad," Number Five Uncle was saying over a mouthful of shrimp dumpling. "We went to a pub near London Bridge, they served roast ham. It was okay – wasn't it?" he appealed to his wife. "Nearly as good as Hong Kong."

"It was," his wife agreed. "Especially with the mustard. But the peas were a bit old. And the chips! As hard as this!" She tapped her chopstick to show how hard the chips were.

"Now, now, you'll put the lad off," Number Five grunted, not wholly pleased. He offered his wife a dumpling, but she was now commiserating with Number Two aunt over her recent trip to London ("It rained all the time!"), and paid him no attention at all.

Number Three aunt took up the challenge. "Siu-ming doesn't have to buy a rice cooker when he's there," she said to his mother, Number Six. "We've got a spare."

"We've got a spare rice cooker as well!" chimed in Number Two aunt. She smiled at Siu-Ming. "You can choose which one you like best!"

She turned to Number Six. "I'm just glad I don't have to go again. So cold. And windy!"

"He's taking lots of soup and instant noodles," said Siu-Ming's mother quickly. "When I was a student in London, that's how I survived."

Here Number Four uncle broke in. "Our son's in London right now, but he won't eat instant noodles. He goes to Chinatown. Young people nowadays...!" He shook his head.

"I don't like instant noodles," Siu-ming said.

"Now, that's not true!" exclaimed his mother. "What about chilli beef and octopus flavour? Just last night!"

"Our son likes noodles here in Hong Kong," Number Four said soothingly. "Just that he won't eat them in London."

Then turning to Siu-ming he said, "The boy's moving back to Hong Kong. He's leaving stuff he doesn't want in our London flat – a bookcase, a coffee-maker, bed-sheets, towels – you name it! Take a look before you buy anything!"

Number One uncle narrowed his grey eyebrows: was Number Four keeping the flat? "Why, yes," said Number Four nervously.

"Well, Siu-Ming can stay there," said Number One. He turned to Number Six. "Problem solved."

"Oh, but our daughter is going to do her Masters in London," Number Four's wife piped up. "She will still be staying in the flat."

Number Four, recovering his nerve, nodded vigorously. Number Six said that Siu-Ming couldn't possibly share with their daughter.

The conversation paused. Number One's grey eyebrows scanned the table, finally reaching Number Five uncle.

Number Five blushed. "Our London tenant has just given notice," he said sheepishly. "Siu-ming can stay in our flat."

"That's very kind!" said Siu-ming's mother. She turned to her son. "You've got a flat now. Number Four will give you their furniture. All you have to do is study!"

"I'm sure we have a down jacket as well," Number Four's wife added, anxious to settle the matter. "It's so cold there, you'll need it!"

The uncles and aunties vied with one another in congratulating Siu-ming on his good fortune. The young man poked at the shrimp dumplings and nodded glumly. The prospect of a year's study loomed before him, but what could he do? He glanced, without much hope, at Number One.

The patriarch, who had been sitting silently through all of this, now turned his grey eyebrows to Number Four. "What is your daughter studying?" he asked.

Number Four smiled glassily. "Ch-chemistry," he stuttered. "Just like Siu-ming."

Number One leant back in his seat, and took out a toothpick. "Problem solved!"

The siblings contemplated this. Siu-ming held his breath.

"But the tickets...!" protested his mother. "I've already bought the tickets!"

"Change the date to December," Number One said. "Take Number Four's daughter out for a Christmas dinner."

There were no more challenges.

At that moment, the roast pork arrived. Siu-Ming took his chopsticks, and picked up a juicy gobbet. Like a prisoner reprieved at the last moment, he contemplated a happy year ahead.

Alchemy of Dust

Linda Kohler

Nothing. Nothing but vines, red dust, and the sun's blue, pink, dark. Nothing but the full sweep of childhood dreams, and a happy sky big enough to contain them. Later, when your body grows to bra, blood and nectar, you grow restless. You sing along with the radio, "we've gotta get out of this place." Every grain in you knows the words are true.

Your father tells you early on how it's done. "You just get in the car and drive, Sweetheart. Like I should have done years ago. There's nothing much here for you. The place is a dead loss."

By then you know the dust. It lines your nostrils and sprays on the back of your hand when you sneeze. It's in your hair, and as much as it falls with the shower water each time you wash, it stays there. You sleep with the dust. It's in your sheets. It's in your throat and in the water you drink. It's the grit of your first kiss, and it glitters your skin. On days when the usual pink shimmer of the air appears clear, you look for it, and you breathe with relief when it washes the onset of night.

For a dead place, it has a lively knack of entering your soul. For a dead place, there's a potent alchemy that jewels the molten days. For a dead place, it leaves a happy stain.

Still, your dad is right. There's nothing much here. So you take the wheel and get the girl out of the dust.

71

After the buzz of the vibrant world and beer has worn off, you find that in most places, the sky is problematic. Obscured by buildings and other big sights. Beautiful places spill with everything, and everything obstructs the view. You can't get it back, that sky that's big enough to hold you.

In Tavira you come close, and you even kiss the dust. But it speaks a language you don't understand. Not quite.

You get your letters, a job, a home that's near water, and you're the first in your family to escape. After a while you get used to the bright lights outside of your window and the narrow streets where the wide, happy sky used to be.

Sometimes, in summer, your busy life settles overnight, and you can taste the dust in the air that blows in through the window screen. You remember its peace. For the next few days your routine is a familiar shade of pink.

When the pink clears, there is nothing that you recognise in your life. Nothing. You see yourself in your work papers, in the Zen of wiping your white kitchen bench and you wonder why it isn't. Zen.

You know what? In the noise, in the clutter and rush, you spend your whole time searching for that holy grail of nothing.

Nothing has stretching space. Nothing lets you breathe. Nothing is gold.

You travel back from time to time, only to find that your father and that old saying are right. "You can never go home." You'd die. No one ever explains to you that you can never leave either. You can't gouge the dust out of your veins. If you tried, you'd die then too.

You want to favour bright lights to grainy stars, but you can't shake the red particles from your inner aesthetic. They are a warm rust in your soul, patina from a time when you bonded with oxygen. Yes, you can wash the dust out of your hair these days, but you can't change the way your strands crave the grains.

There is nothing left but to carry the dust with you. It's heavy sometimes, but you can never unstain yourself because you're born to the dust, you're one with it. You understand it, and nothing else makes sense. Nothing.

Happiness

Kyle Hemmings

Shinjinni drops over in a red halter, purple-rage lipstick, and a pair of Saltwater sandals. She drops the latest CD from Elmore & Wang in my player. It contains the smash dance hit, 'Key Chain Bop Until Yu Drop'. Her ex-boyfriend and my room-mate, Jim, or Jimbo, as she used to call him, gets busy putting on his shoes as he loves to traipse around our apartment with just socks, stitched with pictures of tiny animals. Actually, he's allergic to most species, so he claims.

He's afraid company might disapprove, might wrinkle their noses at the smell, imagined or not, even though Shin is not exactly a stranger. I suspect he hasn't gotten over her–always blushing and stumbling for words whenever she's around. She dumped him for a film student at NYU, five years her junior, and later, he dumped her for a guy named 'Fred', with holes in his jeans and black thick-rimmed glasses. Shin never said much more than that, except that he had a mole on his chin and was into The Godfather movies.

So the three of us are shuffling around the living room, making this crazy train of human links, Shin's hands on Jim's hips, my hands on Shin's, and we're all supposed to kick a leg out, then fall down when Elmore & Wang yell, "NOW DROP THE BOP!"

We fall to the plush orange carpet but we bump our heads together then rub them. It's like chimps imitating one another.

The synchronicity of it makes us laugh and forget the reason we seldom take risks anymore. Our ghost lovers continue to haunt us.

The three of us recline on our backs, looking up at the ceiling, as if it could reveal some new truth. I'm holding Shin's hand and she's locking onto Jim's, which I imagine is sweaty and hot. And I'm finding it peaceful in a strange mystical way, like maybe I'm going to reach some kind of enlightenment about love.

Shin says, "This makes me happy. The three of us just doing stupid things like this, which maybe aren't so stupid. It's like being a child again. The way we used to rest under helicopter trees back in India."

I say, "Yeah, me too. I'll never let you two go. I mean, three is better than one or two."

I didn't mean to sound sentimental, but ONE is the story of my life until Jimbo became a soulmate and Shin proved more perceptive and sincere than the sometimes dizzy and pretentious rich girl from Goa. I'm not even sure she's from Goa. She could be from Bangalore.

Elmore & Wang shout out, "Now do the Key Chain if you want to get laid!"

Jim is quiet. But whether he likes it or not—the three of us are on this key chain and not coming off.

Jim bursts the bubble of silence.

"Anyone mind if I take off my shoes?"

I'm My Own Hero

Walter Giersbach

"I swear, you are the saddest boy I've ever seen," Mom said. "What on earth is wrong?"

Two things made me unhappy. The second was that I didn't know where I came from. "Where am I from? Our teacher told us for homework to find out where we came from."

She said, "Chicago. You were born in Chicago."

"No! I mean, am I English or French or maybe there's some African in me?"

She dried her hands on her apron and got this faraway look she sometimes gets. "Your father would have known about the family tree, but he never wrote anything down. And now he's...." She couldn't bring herself to say again that he had died in Iraq. Losing my Dad was that second reason I was always sad.

The next day my friend Frankie said I should have my DNA checked. He said maybe two percent of us have Neanderthal blood. I've used my Mom's mirror to look at my back and I don't have caveman hair, so I think Frankie was fooling me. But with Dad gone maybe I could find some more of my family.

That night Mom loaned me the money for the DNA test and made me agree to pay her back from my dog-walking job. She helped me send off the check and then I got a package back some time later and I spit into it — the little bottle, not the package — and mailed it back. What a lot of work just to find out who you are!

Well, maybe two months went by and they sent me a report saying I was European. Frankie said Neanderthals lived in Europe, but not any special country unless it was Germany. But .001 percent was "unknown," the paper said. "Huh," I told Frankie, "Maybe some ancestor was from another planet like Superman was."

He ha-ha'ed me. "Yeah, I always thought you looked a little Martian."

Well, that's a bunch of bull-hooey and I told him so. But he'd already told all the kids in our class that I was really a Martian. Being fifth grade morons they all laughed, except Martine, a really good-looking girl who walks to school a long way from where she lives downtown. She and her folks have to live downtown because they're immigrants from someplace like Egypt or one of those countries in the Bible.

Martine and me began talking to each other more, like during lunch period and I got the courage to tell her she had really nice eyes. She told me thank you, and that she was sorry I always seemed sad. But she didn't mention any nice features I had, probably because of the braces on my teeth. About two days later she said, kind of secret like, that guys shout at her and call her names when she walks home to where she lives over a hardware store.

I lied and said she lives near where I have to go and I could walk home with her and have a look. I don't know why people would shout at a nice kid, but it may be 'cause she's different and wears this scarf on her head.

Of course she was right. Two guys who were probably in high school yelled at her to go back to her own country and called her names, like rag head and wetback. I think they were in high school cause they had pimples and really bad acne.

I may be dumb, but I'm not ignorant and my dad always said to face evil head on. So I ran right up to the big guy like I was going to punch him. He kind of swung at me, but I moved behind a stop sign and the kid ran head first into the pole. Blood was coming out of his nose and he sat down hard on his butt. The other not-so-fat kid kind of walked away like he didn't know what was happening.

"You are my hero," Martine said and put her hand on my arm. I felt like the king of the world and said, "Well, he had it coming to him."

"Maybe," she said, "maybe it is a little Neanderthal DNA coming out of you."

No, I told her. "It's actually the Martian in me because I came to earth when I was a little boy and it's my destiny to save people in distress." And you know what she did, I mean right there on Central Avenue? She kissed me on the cheek and said, "You are very handsome when you are happy."

I mean, is that unbelievable? So that DNA test was worth it to discover I was my own hero. It made me happy to think Dad would have been proud.

Ethan's Happy Dance

Tim Philippart

This four-year-old boy, clutching his bear with one hand and mommy with the other, comes into the mom and pop breakfast joint. A table for eight awaits. One seat left for Ann and, probably, a kid's chair, for Ethan. Ethan peeks around mom's ankle length skirt as they burst through the door.

The table wasn't expecting the boy, "Oh, she brought him again."

Seven women turn. Two force weak smiles. Three stare blankly. Two have a look that says, "Why don't you go out the way you came in."

No wonder the kid was hiding in the skirts.

Mommy drags him on over, "I hope you don't mind my bringing Ethan. His daddy had to work overtime this weekend."

Their insincerity drips over every word, "Oh that's fine. We always like to see Ethan. Waitress, bring a chair for the boy."

It is when the boy hears his name from one of the seven that he erupts from the skirts. He is not too loud or too quiet and the restaurant is far from full when Ethan swings into what is, evidently, his version of a happy dance.

Both of Ethan's elbows bend right-angle-upward, as he slides out of mom's grip. Ethan's hands, one gripping the bear, the other with fingers pointing toward the ceiling, make him look like he is an old time preacher, with Bible in hand, about to shout, "Hallelujah," with the bear side, and, "Praise the Lord," with the bare hand.

His legs bend outward at the knees with a right/left crazy cadence. His head is thrown to and fro in sync with the legs.

In a not-too-loud and not-too-quiet voice he semi-shouts, "Mommy bought me some new stuff to keep me quiet and not disturb the ladies while we are here and we are going to unwrap it right now." His voice seemed to change a little when he said "ladies."

Then the weak, the blank, and the dour faces turn to about as genuine smiles as exist these days.

And, I wonder, where did the kid learn to do that?

Did his daddy always do the happy dance when he met mommy at the door?

How about mommy, when the in-laws were coming for supper?

People who meet on the street are seldom happy-dancing.

Maybe, mommy and daddy both do it when the magazine sales guy rings the doorbell?

Wouldn't that be a sight?

What if every country at the next UN meeting did the happy dance?

Suppose Donald and Hillary did it if they got together for old times sake?

When you see me the next time, let's do the dance. Let's see what changes right after that.

Then we can try it with people we don't know or, at least, inside our minds and see what happens then.

No one taught the dance to Ethan. Maybe we knew it once and forgot. Certainly, it couldn't hurt this sad world, if we happy danced, at least, in our hearts.

The Long Happy Life of Carroll Beame

Ruth Z. Deming

Today the little town of Hatboro, PA, has fallen on hard times. Originally, it was named 'Hatborough' and made hats for the Revolutionary War.

You might as well know that I am a curiosity-seeker. And when I see something I like, I investigate. Especially gardens.

The Hatboro post office is like a community center where everyone knows everyone else. Coming out the back door, I saw him! Finally. The gardener I'd been searching for!

Carroll Beame was young then. A mere 85. Looking into his foggy blue eyes, I introduced myself and asked if I could have a tour of his garden. What gardener would refuse?

A magnificent small tree with sweet-smelling purple blossoms stood in the center. I walked over and fondled the leaves.

"What's this?" I asked.

"A wisteria tree," he said in a slightly hoarse voice.

"I thought they only grew as vines," I said.

He explained that if they lived long enough they turned into trees.

I stood and stared as if I were at the Gardens in Luxembourg.

A three-tiered fountain splashed merrily, little rainbows lighting up in the sunshine.

Carroll invited me to sit on his back porch. He asked if I'd like any refreshment. Iced tea for him, a glass of cold water for me.

In the hour or so we chatted, I learned much about his life. He was a hair stylist. He had a huge thatch of blond-gray hair. His former beauty salon had been in front of his house. One of his clients was Florence. He asked for her hand in marriage and she said, "Yes."

His twin sister Caroline lived right around the corner. One day he took me to visit her. She was a suspicious woman who looked me up and down. Apparently, she thought I was going to elope with her then 87-year-old brother.

What a catch!

"Bernice Greenwold has the honor of presenting her daughter, Ruth Zali Deming in marriage to Carroll Beame."

To rub it in, I told her I was Jewish. She probably believed in all the stereotypes about Jews and their lust for money.

We walked back to his house. It towered above the others on the street. I can recall his kitchen with old-fashioned appliances that still worked, though he had to buy a new fridge and a new washing machine that was down in the basement.

I reminded him to walk very carefully up and down the steps, which were very steep.

One day I needed to use the bathroom. I walked carefully up the steep stairway to the second floor, where the restroom was off the master bedroom. Light flooded the room. After peeing, I weighed myself on his scale.

I was always trying to get Carroll to visit my house to see my gardens. He always refused. Too busy.

"Carroll," I said. "How 'bout we go to the coffee shop and I'll treat you to some lunch." This was one of my ruses to show him I wasn't after his money.

We walked over to the Daily Grind. Carroll had a bowl of chicken noodle soup and a Coke, while I had a tuna fish sandwich and a cup of coffee. He told me he was going to stay at his older brother Justice's farm in Maple Glen. Justice, 97, had gone to a nursing home to die.

When I visited, I pulled into the crunchy gravel driveway. There was his shiny black Chrysler Cordoba in the drive. I knocked on the door, while looking at the farm. There was a far-off pond where the cows used to drink. And a chicken coop not far away. By the front door I found some white feathers which I intended to ask if I could have.

I'm a feather collector.

We sat in the kitchen where I had my usual glass of water and he had a glass of iced tea.

"What a lovely place!" I said. "Too bad they're gonna wreck it."

"It's gotta be done," he said, telling me he would stay there until the developers bought the property.

"Will you take me on a tour?" I asked. "I've never seen chicken coops before."

He laughed and said, "They don't smell none too good."

I put the two white feathers in my back pocket and holding his hand, we tottered over the rough terrain to the chicken coop. We ducked inside the low door and the chickens were all around including roosting on the rafters. Although I could barely see them in the darkness, they were attractive animals, looking sort of like cocky bullfighters.

The place smelled foul and I tried not to gag.

Then Carroll showed me a black baby kitten on the outside of the coop. He thought the mother might have died and he was feeding it, hoping she'd come home.

He let me hold it, no bigger than a child's mitten.

We walked back into Justice's house.

I sipped on my cold water, while he told me, not for the first time, where his money would go.

To the Boy Scouts and also the USO of the Army.

"Sounds good," I said. "Don't you have any relatives left?"

"All dead," he said.

That man had no problem about dying. He was certain there was an afterlife and he'd see his beloved Florence in heaven.

Finally, I wrested myself away.

He always liked to kiss me goodbye right on the lips. We kissed goodbye and this is one of the last times I would see him.

Heck, I loved the man.

I saw him one last time before he really got sick. He told me his cat 'Opie' had run away. Had he known death was imminent?

A few months passed and I learned he had died from a couple of strokes. He was 96. His twin sister died a week earlier.

I visited his home and picked up newspapers that had blown into his pink iris on the side of his house. Hard to believe he was gone.

Taking Some Sun

Hannah van Didden

"What are you up to?" The chirpy woman with the grey hair and pink felt hat cast a shadow much longer and leaner than her physical self.

"Sitting. Sit in the flow, take some sun," he said, as if the combination of sitting and sun had a medicinal quality, as though he could take it in a measured dose.

"My name's Veronica. Mind if I sit by you?" She was claiming a place beside him whether he liked it or not, that was clear. The bench creaked with the spread of her hips. She smelled of lavender and, when she opened her mouth, of Earl Grey tea.

"They look after you here?"

"Well enough." He collected his hands at the top of the gnarled walnut walking stick and pushed his shoulders up with his eyebrows.

She grinned and lifted a plastic wallet from her handbag. "See this?" she said. "This is Molly. She was sixteen there. At her deb." He glanced at the photo momentarily. Then he looked away and up at the old building and the prim girls out the front in their starched cotton dresses, his hands still gripped one onto the other.

The woman smiled uncertainly at him and sighed, squelched well-stuck sleeves of plastic off each other until the folded album sprang at her lap like a Jack-in-a-box in reverse.

"And this," she said, turning a leaf. "This one is her with Ethan. Her beau."

He bristled. "Why are you telling me this?"

"Because it's a beautiful story. It was their first date. At her deb." Her eyes twinkled. "You know, from the second their eyes met, they knew they were meant to be." She flicked quickly through the folded leaves until she reached a particular page. "This one. They're getting married, see? Don't they look pleased? Such a proud face he wore. She made a beautiful bride, everyone said. Look. Here. It's us standing by them." Another photo and another. "Their first home. The red walls they wallpapered over. We helped with that, do you remember? And here's one of us when it was all finished. What a sight we were! And here's one of us by the sea."

"Ronnie!" The word escaped him in a warm blast and suddenly he was etching the face from the photo into his fingertips, matching it to the face seated next to him.

"That's right," she breathed. "We were so happy, weren't we?"

"Ronnie, my love, we are that," he said and, gazing down with softer eyes, he squeezed the wrinkled fingers that held the album steady.

She beamed at the top of his tweed hat and returned his gesture. But, by the time he looked to her again, their hands had disconnected, and he was a smiling stranger taking some sun.

Kite

Andrew Grenfell

The string pulls on your hand, tugging urgently like your daughter hauling you by the hand to an ice-cream stand, but this, it's pulling upwards, this red diamond with a curling blue tail, swirling and dipping in the wind.

You lay back on grass thick as dogs' fur, and there's something indefinable in the echoing pure blue above that transports you to your own childhood, somewhere back through so many overgrown tunnels of memory to a beach, cradled by dunes, baking under the blue, sand whistling around your ankles, a battered home-made kite that didn't fly, until an older kid stole it from you and ran, and it rose up rippling behind them, and through your tears your elation that yes, yes it did fly, you just had to run, run as hard as you could, to make more wind, more resistance. Back then, when you had feelings with all the strength of physical forces that couldn't be named, like the stirring in you when your grandmother gathered you in a coarse towel and rubbed your pale and raw body into exhausted dryness, and the future spread endlessly ahead of you, unfathomable, miraculously spooling out day by day. Now you hold it tight, seeking to control, to minimise accidents, to tame the erratic, the unpredictable, the dangerous.

You unwind more string and the kite gratefully rises higher, the white noise of flapping waning, faint, riding the high breeze unburdened but for this tenuous link you control. You blink and turn your head: there is your daughter who spurned this mythic experience – it's okay, your annoyance at her disinterest has already dissipated (you're already back to practising patience), and you tell yourself that even though you didn't share this kite moment with her, you'll share some other moment that will slide into the folklore of your shared memories like a sheet of patterned paper into an old filing cabinet. She totters on the lush green, chasing something only she can see, pink hat flopping, unconcerned with the mothers walking prams, the boisterous boys playing ball games, the elaborate picnics, the trees like swaying sentinels lining the lazy river. Your wife stands alone, laughing at your daughter, white cotton dress fluttering around her slight figure; a hand shades her eyes. What is she thinking, this person who has become as mysterious and untouchable as an ocean wave, this person who you once needed so much it made you ache. And even though you tell yourselves you're somehow managing it, together, this strange new life of parenting, of days patched close, you wonder how life's borders narrowed even as they widened: you used to talk about art, for goodness sake! And philosophy, and existentialist literature (is there any other kind?); but those days of bohemian disposition, of Marxist experiment, of fluidly shifting relationships have long receded, diminished in the rear-view of your hopes and dreams: they seem laughable now, in this park of noisy prosaic play.

The kite pulls again, harder. It could equally be a struggling silver fish straining a fishing line... how you love that unthinking pull of nature... and the time that had stopped for an instant rushes forward again, insistently, and you imagine – you imagine the wild sky teeming with kites, hundreds, perhaps thousands, a panoply of colours vivid and rushed and busy. And though you know the weather of your marriage is souring, that when you have sex with your wife it's merely a release of predictable lust (she gives herself ironically now, if at all), and you snipe blindly at each other, what you don't know is that the inexorable continental drift of a dynamic neither of you can rebuff will soon leave you at opposite poles; you'll forge different lives and your daughter will be caught like flotsam in the eddies of your wake. But that untidiness is still months away. Right now you're tethered in this moment, and it's something to lie here and know peace, perhaps even happiness; to feel the sun like strong hands on your face; to tiptoe around the edges of who you are, this kite-holder, who still feels something, at least.

The banal shrouds of clouds convene, and you gather up your few belongings. You grip the corner of the kite's sure geometry as you leave the park, all holding hands. Your drifting mind knows your journey has become uncertain, beset with doubt, happiness only possible in the gaps of a widening alienation; and wonders, too, if the kite is your daughter, or your wife, or you: it is a long way home.

The Cherry Brandy Fiasco

Arthur Black

Unlike my mother, whose warm charisma and sense of humor attracted friends like an electromagnet, my father preferred to remain a lone wolf of sorts. People liked him, but they didn't gravitate to him as they did to my mother. Aside from his brothers, my father had only two close friends, the Lombardi brothers, Carlo and Gianni, who lived across the street from us. Although my father grew up in Russia, thousands of miles from the Sicilian birthplace of the Lombardi brothers, and even though they spoke different languages and followed different religions, the three men formed a strong bond. From the shards of their broken English, they pieced together a way to communicate with each other. My mother had a simple explanation for their warm relationship: "They're all three of them crazy."

"You can call us crazy if you want," my father said. "But it makes us happy to do things together."

My father rarely drank much alcohol, but he liked making wine with the Lombardi brothers. Carlo and Gianni owned a wine press, which they set up in my father's garage. The three men would drive to a railroad siding nearby and buy huge amounts of grapes shipped in from vineyards in California. Then they would spend hours talking and laughing while they crushed the grapes in the wine press and poured the juice into wooden barrels mounted on the X-shaped sawhorses that my father built in his basement workshop.

When the right time came, my father would bring six bottles of deep-red wine from the garage into the house. He would give two bottles to each of my uncles and keep two for himself. The rest of the bottled wine went to the Lombardi brothers.

One year, after the railroad cars from California had arrived with fresh loads of fruit, the Lombardi brothers proposed making something different. Instead of wine, they thirsted for cherry brandy.

Once again, Carlo and Gianni set up their wine press in my father's garage, but this time they used it to crush loads of cherries instead of grapes. All seemed to go well until one evening at dinnertime when a tremendous explosion in the garage interrupted our meal. The blast rattled all the windows of our house, and I thought that the roof would cave in on us.

My father had just bought a new car, and he feared that some manufacturing defect had caused it to blow itself up. He raced to the garage. My mother, Morris, and I, ran right behind him, all of us afraid that we would find our new car totally destroyed. But, yippee! It had remained intact. However, the color of the car seemed to have changed from brown to red. The sweet smell of cherries hung heavy in the air, and cherry pulp covered everything inside the garage — ceiling, walls, floor, garden tools, the new car — everything.

My mother went to get a broom and a mop for my father to clean up the mess. While we awaited her return, he tiptoed through the thick red mush on the floor to inspect the car. The brandy makers had not pitted the cherries they put into the wine press, and the stones had shot out of the demolished barrels like shrapnel blasted from a bomb. Dozens of pits were embedded in the soggy mess dripping down the side of the car.

My father scraped off some of pulp on the left rear passenger door and ran his fingers across the metal. My brother and I stopped laughing and held our breath. Thanks to the heavy steel and thick lacquer paint that automakers used back then, the bright finish of our new car had weathered the cherry pit bombardment without a single ding.

It took hours to remove the cherry pulp from the garage. My father had to use a garden hose to wash the place down. He shoveled most of the red mash into buckets, which he emptied on the earth surrounding the rose bushes in the garden. He claimed that pulverized cherries would make good fertilizer.

The next day, the Lombardi brothers came over to pick up what remained of their wine barrels. My mother listened patiently while they tried to explain what went wrong.

In their broken English, the brothers said that perhaps they had put too much sugar in the barrels, or, for all they knew, not enough. Maybe they had put in too much yeast, or, possibly, too little. In any case, they had done *something* wrong. They apologized for the trouble they caused and solemnly promised that it would never happen again. My mother graciously accepted their apology, but she made it clear that my father's career as a winemaker had come to an end. This didn't upset my father. He had a new project in mind: he wanted to replace the wooden doors of the garage with ones made of steel. That night, humming happily, he began making sketches of the metal doors that he spent the next three months building and assembling with the help of the Lombardi brothers.

Not in my genes

Kate Mahony

I come from a family who like playing tricks on people. I don't mind practical jokes as a rule – I laugh at those lame April Fools jokes at work – but the thing with my family is their pranks aren't actually funny. They're often retaliation for old grievances. Ongoing battles carried out by people who have iron wills when it comes to finding ways to fight back.

Scarcely a month goes by without my being told of this prank or that. Like putting up a fake billboard showing someone's house for sale at a much reduced price. Listing the first Open Home so it is due to start around the time they arrive back tired and jetlagged from a trip overseas.

Last time, my brother was relaying details of yet another wind-up, I said, "That is not funny. Seriously. It's cruel and insensitive." And then I got into the spirit of it and added heatedly, "Manipulative and deceitful." As I said this, I thought how glad I was to have skipped the gene for recrimination.

He said back, "I guess it is a different sense of humour. Just a fun thing. People like to be happy, you know."

After I put the phone down, I thought about this. I began to wonder if all along, the rest of my family had me down as some boorish person lacking any sense of fun. I could just see them now, gathering without me, around the fireplace at one of their houses, drinking beer and eating pretzels. Mocking me. Making jokes at my expense.

I felt annoyed. I grew angry. I didn't calm down all evening. I sat there in my chilly living room determined to think of some trick I could play on them. Something equally cruel and meaningless. I would wait till I was sure it had worked and they were sufficiently angry and uncomfortable.

Then I would phone each of them in turn and ask, "Are you happy now?"

That would show them.

Geisha

Robert Scotellaro

He puts an ad in the paper for a geisha. It is the wet, mushy center of a New York summer, and she arrives breezy at his door in a gauzy outfit. Her face is zombie-white with greasepaint contrasting candy apple-red lipstick. When he requests a fan dance, she grabs up a small electric fan from the kitchen table. Asks if he has an extension cord, which he does. She has him take off his trousers and lie down on the couch in his tighty-whities. She edges up close, with a little hip wiggle and shoulder roll, and runs the frisky air up and down him. Sings a Lady Gaga song he doesn't recognize, and dances to it.

* * *

For the tea ceremony, she uses Lipton while he waits so long for it to chill in the frosted glasses from the freezer that he turns on the TV and watches the news. They sit on the couch and drink it. Make several toasts back and forth, the ice cubes nearly spilling over the top. She, continually filling his glass every time it lowers an inch or two. And he, excusing himself to go to 'the little boy's room'.

* * *

When asked to read him some poetry, she bows and recites a couple of dirty limericks she used to hear her drunken father recite, with a slurred and salacious bravado at family get-togethers.

*   *   *

He is happy to see she is comely when she steps from the bathroom with her make-up off, and is delighted to find she likes a lot of the same TV shows he does. Later in the evening, they perform fan dances for each other to his Elvis records. Only once, when they become overly adventurous, pulling the plug from the wall.

Seventeen

Jill Kiesow

They had always said money couldn't buy happiness.

They were wrong.

Cassandra Sumner links her hands together and stretches her arms over her head. Twenty-eight years and she hasn't let her arms go soft. She slides open the glass door, clicks black high heels onto the patio and, placing her hands on the railing, looks out over Atlanta.

To say Cassandra's beginnings had been humble would be an understatement. Her past was rotten, tumbling, reeking of the decay that comes with even the most careful life lived in desperate poverty, even while she cleaned incessantly and bedsheets snapped in the wind. There was something in the air that had sensed the weakness that came with destitution, some hidden force that caused dry rot and mildew to appear where it wouldn't otherwise.

As she walked without destination that day, her threadbare calico dress seemed to be fading more by the minute under the hot sun. Her bare feet and large straw hat added insult to injury. She was a walking cliché. She strongly considered the other option – nudity – and she may have done it. But just before her heat-swollen fingers reached for the top button, as sweat threatened to make mud of the dirt under her feet, he drove by, slowed, stopped. When he leaned across the bench seat and pushed open the door, the miracle of air conditioning burst into the heat, and she caught sight of a face more handsome than any she'd seen before. She didn't hesitate to slide in. Her ratty straw hat took the brunt of the Cadillac's exhaust as she tossed it onto the lane, to be picked up by someone needier than herself. Someone who was trapped there. Cassandra slammed the door, the car peeled out, and covered the whole of that tiny Georgia town in dust.

*　　*　　*

Never did Cassandra ever expect Jake would be the one. He was what he was: a ride, a ticket. A portal. She hadn't left anyone behind, no one that was anything more than a memory and a grassy mound in the churchyard outside the limits of that old town she'd all but forgotten. Before she could join them, he'd taken her away, and that was all she'd wanted from him.

Then there were the others. One gave her silicone boobs, one gave her his name, one gave her society. She gave them her virginity, her youth, her time and patience.

She didn't stay seventeen forever, though those salad days did last more than a few years, or so she said, when she discovered the magic of that word, "seventeen".

*　　*　　*

Another hotel room. This one was going for mid-century modern but missed vintage altogether and came off looking cheap and used. The horrid gold curtains drawn against the day let in sunlit melancholy, allowed too many long shadows, exposed self-deprecation.

Cassandra sat, legs crossed, half-dressed, TV muted, in the gloom. Her purse was flung on the loveseat. There was no

98

overnight bag. She knocked cigarette ash into a coffee cup, not the cup of gin.

"I've done it a million times," he'd said, zipping, buttoning. It didn't matter who he was. It was always the same.

"Your wife must know."

"So?"

On his way out, head stuck back in through the door, he reminded her of check-out time but he needn't have bothered. She'd be gone. She always was.

*   *   *

Cassandra smooths her hands down her leggings, conscious of her strong thighs under the thin fabric. Now it is yoga, Pilates, personal trainers to keep her aging body as fit as she used to be from hard work alone. For years she'd been the wife who knows, whose husbands didn't care that she knew. She lights a cigarette and wonders.

Would she have been happier if she'd stayed in that past life, kneeling by her mama's grave with weedy wildflowers in her hand and insincerity in her heart? She doesn't think so. Would she have been happier being a mama herself? No. She'd become too selfish to destroy her body and give her time to a dependent. Her gauzy shirt flaps in the breeze, slips down over one shoulder. Would she have been happier had one of the husbands stayed? Hell no. As it is, she's waiting for the old coot in the master bedroom to succumb to old age or pneumonia or coronary failure. He isn't cognitive enough to know she sleeps in the guest room, when she sleeps at home.

He summons her now, ringing the accursed pewter bell. She ignores it until she finishes her smoke and crushes it out in the crystal ashtray. She re-enters the cool condo, closing the door on the heat and humidity. The thick ivory and mauve Oriental rug muffles her heels. She sinks into luxury.

"Coming, darling," she hollers so he can hear. The volume makes her voice lose its fake sweetness.

He rings the bell again.

"Just a minute, love." Before going to his bedside, Cassandra slips into the guest room. On her knees in the back corner of the walk-in closet, she reaches and extracts a beautifully decorated box. Sitting back, she lifts the lid and carefully lifts out a small piece of calico fabric. The rest of the dress is long gone. Here it is, her past in her hands. She holds it toward the window and can see daylight through the ragged fabric.

The bell rings again, accompanied by grunting as he tries to call out to her. She replaces the fabric, returns the box.

"Coming, sweetheart." She stands and walks briskly toward the master suite. She passes through tasteful pastel rooms, decorated to her liking, not his. She's not the one leaving. It's modern, simple, clean. She runs a hand over the pale blue settee and smiles. Would she have done anything differently? No. It's gone according to plan. She has everything she ever wanted. She couldn't be any happier.

Without God
There Is Nothing

J. Bradley

Kafka and the ocean wed on a Monday. The invitations were in the shape of a swordfish, something they both agreed represented the best of both of them.

At the reception, Kafka carved another piece from the moon and fed it to the ocean. *This will be the last time*, he promised. The ocean smashed the remaining piece of the moon between Kafka's teeth.

The ocean washed away the leftover moondust in the honeymoon suite. As Kafka fell asleep, he asked The Lord for his fleshy fingers and arms back.

Eulogy

Melisa Quigley

He read until he couldn't anymore. He had cataracts and refused to have them operated on. His eyes were cloudy white pearls, which made him look creepy. He refused to use a walking stick or walker because he said they were for old people. Every time we spoke to him we would have to shout because he wouldn't wear a hearing aid. He had a very strong grip of my arm and would shuffle one foot in front of the other and tell me stuff that he thought was important.

"You'll never get what you want in life. You'll always have to settle for second best," he said.

To prove his point, he would hold a lolly in each hand and put them behind his back and ask me to pick which one I wanted and give me the other lolly.

Grandpa Eli was a man of many words and was always right. No one ever challenged his views unless they wanted an argument. He was 93 when he died and relived the war like he was ready to do battle at any moment. His medals hung off his food-stained jacket and he always spoke about the people and places in the war. He had a headdress from Papua New Guinea that he let me try on, but only if I put it back on the wall in the living room where it hung.

Grandpa Eli never had a kind word to say about anyone. He was a racist. He hated every nationality except Australians even though Australia is a multi-cultural society. His ancestors were English on his mum's side and Scottish on his father's. Nobody knew where Grandpa Eli was born because his parents died before Dad got to meet them. Some relatives said a garbo found him beside a rubbish bin and felt sorry for him and took him home. I believed this to be true.

At Christmas, Grandpa Eli couldn't wait for everyone to unwrap their presents so he could collect all the paper in a big plastic bag. Even after dinner he'd throw all the leftovers in the kitchen bin and take it outside and empty it into the garbage. He used to say cleanliness is next to Godliness even though he wasn't religious.

As a child, he'd visit the Victoria Market and fossick through the rubbish for something to eat. If Grandpa stood side on he'd appear like a crooked stick. He hated fat people and considered them lazy. His motto was sitting around never made anyone wealthy.

I went to a Catholic Primary School and told him I wanted to be a priest when I grew up.

"You don't want to be a poofter," said Grandpa Eli.

I used to play with marbles and my teacher thought I was more interested in playing than learning and spoke to Mum about it.

"So long as he doesn't lose his marbles like his grandfather has, I don't really care," said Mum.

When I was eight, my parents used to go away on weekends and drop me off at my grandparents. Grandpa Eli used to sit at the kitchen table and pull his false teeth in and out of his mouth and Grandma would rinse her teeth under the cold tap after she'd eaten and put them down her stockings for safekeeping. Whenever I tried to pull my teeth out they stayed in my jaw and my grandparents would laugh at me.

He told me I should work as a barber because everyone needed a haircut and I'd make lots of money. Being on my feet all day would keep me skinny. My happiest memory was helping him feed his birds. He had an aviary with fifty canaries and knew each one by name and would talk to them. Afterwards, we'd have a beer and he'd tell me it would put hairs on my chest. Grandma scolded him and told him he should've mixed the beer with lemonade but he acted like she hadn't spoken. He'd sit in his favourite chair in the living room, a recliner with footrest, and stare vacantly in front of him. His eyes closed and his mouth opened to a low snore. I loved Grandpa Eli. We were very similar but as I grew older I preferred wine to beer and I don't take prescription medication.

He liked me when I was a child, but embarrassed me when I turned eighteen and Mum introduced him to my girlfriend at a family function. My girlfriend wore a low-cut blouse and Grandpa Eli called her a slut to her face. She never saw me after that and I refused to have anything to do with him for several years.

Even though our family stood by Grandpa Eli and kept in contact with him, he left everything to charity. At the funeral, the only mourners were my parents and me. Friends and relatives sent condolences but failed to attend even though the arrangements were in the paper.

At times, during the service, I felt like I was floating in the air watching the world go by, stifled because I was disconnected from everyone. I sat with my parents in the church and listened to the priest and repeated everything after him.

"God our Father, Your power brings us birth…" I'd heard his prayers so many times before. I could say them in my sleep.

Later, we stood at Grandpa Eli's grave and the priest said Grandpa was up with God now. The clouds parted and the sun shone but didn't warm me. I felt numb. Mum's new court shoes hurt her feet and I overheard her ask Dad if we could go home soon.

We had a cup of tea back at our house and a neighbour visited who used to get Grandpa Eli's prescription medication.

"You know your grandpa was very proud of you, James," said the neighbour. "He said that you were good at cutting his hair."

Gym Out

Mbeke Waseme

I'm tired of trying to see the good in all people. I stood at the counter, having handed the three-day free pass printout to the male attendant I had seen last week and although he thought that he recognised me, he said nothing. He had this semi-anxious look on his face that I had noted when I first met him. He didn't respond but instead handed the form to the older lady next to him. She looked at me too... for a little too long, I thought.

"Have you been here before?" she asked.

"I haven't," I lied.

She looked at me again and called someone, somewhere. I could hear her spelling my name out. The yoga teacher walked by and smiled at the attendant and at me. I tried not to make it look as if we had already met. I had enjoyed her aerial yoga class so much that I thought, if I could get another three days free, I would sign up for the package next week when I got paid. After all, that eight-day pass that Rajita had given me at work, that shouldn't count, as this was my first online application for a free pass. And, I had not been able to attend all eight days due to work commitments, so technically, I was owed the three days that I had lost.

I looked at the clock. It was 10.35. If I could move quickly, I could change and be in the room for the 10.45 start. I really should have worn my yoga pants under my dress to save time.

"Would you like to see a manager?" the attendant asked

"Of course," I responded with much enthusiasm. "I would love to see the manager as I plan to join the gym but I really wanted to try out this aerial yoga class so could I see the manager after the class?"

"OK. You'd like to do the aerial yoga class and see the manger afterwards?"

I so hated the way people in this region repeated whole sentences back to me. I remained calm and responded, "Yes. Yes." It was now 10.39.

"OK!" she said and began to get my towels and locker key. I turned to check the messages on my phone when I heard, "Hi there, how were the classes last week?" I looked up to see one of the overly helpful managers I had met after the Saturday advanced yoga class. He looked at my free pass in the attendant's hand and looked at me. The attendant had a funny and confused look on her face. She had aged by 5 or so years.

"You can't have another free pass, madam. This is for first time users only!" the overly helpful manager said.

I wanted to tell him how happy I felt as a first-time user. How the introductory classes to aerial yoga had been so fabulous that I wanted some more of that adrenaline rush and needed it to help me get through the day. To let him know that I was a creative, currently working on projects and very much needing to be in the space with that awesome teacher who gave me real feedback. A teacher who was so unlike the terrible Sergeant major of a yoga teacher who worked in my condo and who ignored me throughout the class, making a point of only touching the Chinese and white students.

She touched and praised no brown students, no matter how good we were. In the last class of hers that I had attended, as I stood there in standing extended leg stretch, begging her to 'look at me miss. Look at me,' I realised how I had craved her validation and how much she was unable to give it me. The one Chinese woman with whom I had connected in that class had clocked the scenario and had mouthed 'it's really good' to the wounded mini-me standing there. I had left vowing not to return for I was worthy of more and knew that as great as my practise was, she should not be the person I should look to for that confirmation.

I had attended other classes since living in Malaysia, with teachers who sat fixing their lipstick and hair in the mirrors after they had given instructions for the asanas. I had attended classes where teachers chatted to their friends whilst we died a little more trying our best to hold the poses, and sometimes had to simply collapse as the teacher's attention had long left the students who came to the class. No, this teacher was different and my brown skin was not a deterrent to her. She had walked over to me and had adjusted me with love and care. She wanted me to be the best I could be. After one class, she had asked, "Have you done aerial yoga before?" and I was super proud to say, "no, this is my second class" and to hear her respond with "you're really good."

"If you are interested in joining, we can sit over here and I can go through the options with you," said the overly helpful attendant. We moved to the seated area and the attendants watched as I was led away. I looked up at the clock. It was 10.46 and I knew that she would have started. The manager went on about the 4-month and the 12-month packages which were available. I could only join using a credit card and not my debit card. He wondered how flexible my job was as he had seen me there at 10.30am last week. I explained that it made more sense to do an early class. To not have a lunch break. To avoid the mad evening traffic. To utilise the Uber and Grab special offers which always began at 10.00am.

He looked puzzled.

I wondered why I was still there.

At 11.00am I left.

First Date

Peter Lingard

"It was a strange evening. Oh, he was turned out nicely enough; darkish grey suit with a black shirt and tie. He smelled good. And he looked good; those gorgeous eyebrows. I've shown you his picture, right? He has great eyebrows. He was a good talker and his voice… I felt the timbre of his voice in my body. I mean, he'd say some words and I swear the table vibrated. I kept my leg in contact with the table leg throughout the meal. To give him his due, he was a good listener. He barracks for The Crows, but I can get past that. He apparently works at a brokerage house and earns a decent amount. He says he's never been married and has no kids, so that's good. Don't pull that face, the strange part is coming.

'I'm glad you didn't ask about walks along the shore and picnics in the park in your come-on,' he said. 'They're lovely ideas but basically they're desperate attempts by people to appear romantic. A good sense of humour is what's paramount in a relationship.'

The food was good. I had garlic snails for my entrée. Stop looking like that! If he wanted to kiss me it was up to him to order something with garlic; which he did – garlic prawns. That made me happy. Anyhow, I had roast duck with cherry sauce for mains while he ate an enormous rare steak with salad. We shared a good Merlot. I have the name and vintage in my bag and I'll give you the details later. I told him about me, well, all he needed to know at this point; just a more detailed account of what's already in my profile, really.

The date was going well until he proposed. I laughed aloud and his eyes lit up and a satisfied grin appeared on his face. This is the strange part, as if I had to tell you. He said he proposes to all first dates that are at or above his requirement levels. Arrogant I know, but, that voice and the eyebrows... Apparently, those he still finds interesting when pudding's served are honoured with his proposal. He told me later that those who, like me, don't want a dessert are urged to have a coffee, tea, or a cognac; not brandy, cognac. So I had cognac, naturally. Women who turn shy or walk out are forgotten, those who say 'of course' are possibles, and those who laugh are definite prospects. It's his way of finding out how sincere they are about requiring a GSOH in the men they seek. 'It cuts down the field,' he said. Anyway, two can play his game. I'm seeing him again on Friday when I'll inform him it's the wedding night. Remind me to book a room at the Hyatt tomorrow. I want to see if he can put a happy smile on my face. But I'm telling you, if *he* laughs, he dies."

Aardboy

E. M. Stormo

Aardboy lived on a farm. The family called it a farm, but it was more of a compound, and the family was more of a cult. Aardboy wasn't exactly a boy either, but there were other boys around to compare him to.

The compound was sometimes called a camp, because it had a swimming pool, a library, and an orchestra. Aardboy swam in the morning, read a book in the day, and listened to an evening concert. He did all of these things until someone in the family needed his nose.

Then he'd be down in the aard, digging a trench and rooting through it. His methods were opaque to the family and yet he always yielded results. Once finished, he'd let them know with a particular snort. Someone would inspect his choice of aard and give him a pat on the head. Then it was time to shape the aard, thick reddish brown like cinnamon on an oatmeal breakfast. He wanted to consume it on the spot, but the aard wasn't for him, so he rolled it smooth and spherical, and passed it on for whatever purpose the family had in mind.

The boys bathed and fed him afterwards. That was their one job on the compound, and they worked with a whistle and a smile. They spent a few hours to get him clean enough for the pool. The rest of the time the boys used to play around the compound. They never went to the concerts or the library.

Between his aard-rolling and boy-bathing, the family named him Aardboy. The boys weren't quite family, and the aard wasn't quite home. And Aardboy was nothing more than farm equipment—an irreplaceable piece of farm equipment, stored alongside the others in the barn, but even the weapons stockpile was given its own shelf to sit upon.

To Aardboy, the boys were on equal ground with the aard itself. He also viewed himself as a piece of aard, equally shaped by the grounds of aard and boy. But the family were gods, coming and going at the speed of light. They moved as one so it was hard to distinguish between them, although one of them, the head of the family, went out of his way to distinguish himself to Aardboy.

Aardboy would be rooting around aimlessly when the head of the family arrived from nowhere. Before Aardboy could turn his head upwards to see, the man was right in front of his nose. He inspected Aardboy himself at least once a week. Nice bridge. Straight sinuses. The usual wear and tear from usage. But the skin inside Aardboy's left nostril had softened. He only noticed the problem when he thumbed inside.

Aardboy wouldn't admit the truth at first, but after the promise of extra house privileges, the incident came out. A boy purposely hooked him by the nostril during a recent bath. Such boys were disciplined one time only.

The family used their light-magic on him and made sure all the other boys watched. Aardboy was invited to watch too. The whole family was there, and the head personally thanked him for his service, which the boys had trouble making sense of. He told them Aardboy is able to detect a faint scent of a certain mineral found here on the South African coast. It helps create a black hole for the family to live in, safe from the spooks. The hole is the family's home. The spooks can't see in the hole, although there is light inside. The boys didn't believe it but the Hole Theory sounded plausible to Aardboy's mind.

When they were finished, the family left the boy in the aard. Aardboy was happy for a new aardboy to play with, if only for a night. He skipped the concert to play. The two aardboys became best friends, until the next day when he rolled the other aardboy over to the pond, because it's okay to leave a boy in the pond—nothing there tastes good anyway. The aard, however, should be kept fresh as breakfast and smelling of cinnamon. Free of boys and free of family. Then he could follow the iridescent trail home to his own black hole where nobody would see.

Morning Story

Scott Hughes

The old man awoke to find at his bedside a beautiful woman with hair and skin that glowed as if made of moonlight. Although she looked familiar, he didn't know her, but he did know she was no ordinary woman—a witch or fairy, perhaps. He sat up to demand she tell him who she was and where they were… and who he was. Before he could speak, though, he noticed tears in her eyes.

"Good morning," she said, resting her shining hand on his pale, wrinkled one. With her other hand, she wiped her eyes.

"Morning." The old man started to get out of bed, his joints popping in protest.

"You mustn't," said the lady. "You don't have much energy." She put her hands on his arms to keep him from getting up. "Lie down."

Grumbling, he did as she instructed.

"Are you going to tell me what's going on here?" he asked. "Who are you? Where are we?"

"I'm someone who loves you deeply," she answered. "And you're home."

"Home?" The old man couldn't believe someone this beautiful—human, witch, or otherwise—would love a shriveled old grouch like him. "I don't remember this place. I don't even remember who I am."

She gestured to a nearby shelf that held dozens of books. "You are the one who filled these pages with stories."

"I wrote all those?" The old man's eyes grew wide. "Will you… read one to me?"

Glimmering like a star, the lady took a dusty, tattered book from the shelf. She opened it and read about a princess trapped in a dark cave by a goblin. A young prince—the son of her father's greatest enemy—rescued her, and their marriage ended their families' feuding.

When she finished reading, the old man wanted to hear another story. He enjoyed the tale, yes, but mostly he loved listening to the lady's soothing voice—like a cool hand on your neck after a hot day spent toiling in the fields. She read to him, story after story of fearless knights and enchanted stones, until the setting sun's orange light filled the house.

She put away the book, and the old man closed his eyes. The lady touched his cheek.

"Rest now," she said.

"One more story," he said.

She chose another book and opened it, but as she began this story she did not need to read the words from the pages— she knew it by heart. In this story a farmer's son became lost in a dark forest and happened upon a beautiful tree nymph just as she was breathing life back into a dead tree. She agreed to lead him back home if he told her a story. The life of a tree nymph, she told him, was quite uneventful, and hearing a fascinating story from a human boy would be delightful. As they strolled through the forest, the boy told her of growing up a farmer's son—planting and harvesting crops, tending to the animals— and the tree nymph was captivated. When they reached the forest's edge, the nymph said she couldn't leave the woods. She kissed the boy quickly, then retreated to the trees, giggling. The boy could still feel the kiss on his lips when he arrived home.

Every day the boy returned to the forest to follow the nymph and tell her stories as she went around reviving lifeless trees. His stories grew more imaginative, and the nymph loved hearing his tales of elf kings and scheming imps and talking animals. Soon they fell in love, and the boy came to live with her in the woods. He spent his days writing wondrous stories, and the nymph never tired of hearing or reading them. As the years passed, the boy grew older and older still, yet the tree nymph remained as young and beautiful as the first day they'd met. Then one day the farmer's son, now an old man, knew his days were coming to an end. He did not want to leave the nymph, so he asked her to use her powers to bring him back to life like a tree in the forest.

As the lady finished the story, the old man again saw tears in her eyes.

"That one I didn't make up, did I?" he said.

She shook her head.

"So I will die tonight," he said.

She nodded.

"And when you bring me back to life tomorrow, I won't remember any of this."

She shook her head. Then she stared out the window at the moonlight coating all the trees in a veneer of silver. "I'll continue until the day you tell me to stop."

The old man thought for a time, then said, "Don't forget to read me the story of the farmer's son tomorrow. It's my favorite."

The woman turned back to him, smiling. "Mine, too."

He held out one of his frail hands, and the lady—the young, radiant nymph—took his hand in hers. In that moment, her touch made him feel that he could go on living forever without her magic.

"Rest now," said the nymph. "I'll see you in the morning."

The old man lay back and closed his eyes. Even though he wouldn't recognize her tomorrow, he knew a deep part of him would never forget her, never let her go. As he drifted into sleep he dreamt of the beautiful glowing face that would greet him and the shining arms that would embrace him when he awoke in the morning.

Red for Love

Prospero Pulma Jr.

"It was love. Love." It is her sixth visit. The words ring like the chorus of an unforgettable song. Her words are also on the lips of the high school girls, college girls, girls out of school, young women, even mothers who visit us. They all say love spurs them to act. The words are as universal as the deed that leads them to us. Regardless of the branch of life and layer of society they are in, they come to us for that deed.

I want to dare them to claim that their deed is an act of love while holding a mirror to their faces. I wonder if their love stems from tearing what has thousands of sunsets and sunrises in store for it if only it remains whole, if only they are willing to lose, to gain more than their bodies and dreams, if only my peers and I are not their professional accomplices – nay, enablers!

"For love?" I mutter. Those years of dismembering what is full and thriving now weigh like a mountain in my mind. My profession wears white. I now believe the hangman's mask suits me better.

"For love."

The steel in her voice shot straight into the years of black snow on that mountain.

I dump her chart on her bed. "Then your mother must hate you so."

119

She looks at me with eyes that are about to crack. She does not need a mirror. Neither do I.

I tear off my scrub suit and fling it to the floor. The black mountain of my past and present can shake loose its dirt to smother me, but I want it to bury me happy in the sun, not here in this dark sterile environment. I want to smile and laugh with mirth.

The Beginning of the End of a Ladies Man

Brian Obiri-Asare

For all intents and purposes I no longer exist. I'm dead to the world today. I've switched off my phone, I've hidden my laptop under my bed, if anyone bothers buzzing my apartment I won't answer, I'll continue sitting here on the couch with a pack of cigarettes and a bottle of whiskey beside me. When nighttime comes I won't turn on the lights. I've closed all the blinds so people will think I'm not home. I won't turn on the TV, I won't listen to music, I won't move, I won't eat. For all intents and purposes I no longer exist. I can't imagine how I'm going to share the news. Over coffee? Over a beer? Ever since Monday, when the doctor called and said we needed to speak in person, I've been trying to get used to the idea that I no longer exist. Not the old me. Not anymore. A few years back, I was clicking my way through a YouTube rabbit hole when I stumbled across a doco about AIDS. Skinny Africans who didn't bother wearing condoms wasting away. Somewhere in the back of my mind I knew they were fucked but not how. I guess I'm now going to find out how, way sooner than I ever imagined.

*   *   *

As difficult as things are now, they are only going to get worse, because this is only the beginning. I don't feel any pain yet, I only feel numb. The doctor was completely shocked I hadn't come to see him earlier. When you took a shower for example, he said, didn't you notice any changes to your body? Didn't you notice the sores, the weight loss? When I say nothing. his eyes whisper to me, *This is the end.*

The breast pocket of his white shirt was stained with a patch of blue ink. His spidery, latex-glove hands examined my body, from top to bottom, meticulously. Now and then, as he examined me in deathly silence, he nodded. To himself. The nurse beside him nodded when he nodded, her eyes also whispering, *This is the end.*

Outside the hospital patients walked to and fro and around in circles. Sickly humans in pyjamas, their eyes different from healthy human eyes. Like the eyes of the skinny Africans who didn't bother wearing condoms wasting away on the doco I saw on YouTube and never really cared about at the time. What has always freaked me out about sick people is the whisper of death in their eyes. I looked at my self in the mirror yesterday and I could see the same whisper. Yes, it looked like my usual face – no thinner, no more anxious, just my usual face, a little downcast, a little dishevelled, slightly pale, my big nose just like my mother's – but the whisper was unmistakable. When I think of all the people I've slept with recently, inside the last six months, I wonder if the same whisper exists in their eyes. But then again, maybe like me they no longer exist.

* * *

With no phone, no music, no laptop, no contact with the outside world, I don't know what to make of my apartment. I look around and notice the furniture, I notice the paintings, I notice the record player, the speakers, I notice the TV, I notice the shag rug, like a permanent dark stain. I notice my legs too, wasting away. Another couple of hours and all this will disappear into total darkness – the furniture, the paintings, the record player, the TV, the speakers, the rug and me. I'm not hungry. I'm not thirsty. I'm not happy. I'm not sad, only numb. There are some mangoes in the fridge. They are in season and I like the taste of cold mangoes, the sweetness of their juicy flesh. I cut off the cheeks and then cut up the flesh on each cheek into little squares, and then eat them, one by one. I've done that for as long as I can remember, ever since I was a little kid. I never have been a fan of the flesh remaining on the seed. To this day, I can't get my head around how an entire mango tree can grow from a seed, how there is a whole embryonic tree inside, ready to grow. While the doctor was examining me, that was what came to mind, not death or AIDS, but the magic of a sweet and juicy mango somehow emerging from a seed. It seems almost uncanny. The mangoes are wasting away inside the fridge, bruised and wounded, just like me, just like the skinny Africans on the doco I saw on YouTube.

Anyways, enough with mangoes. I'm dead to the world today. I'll continue sitting here on the couch with a packet of cigarettes and a bottle of whiskey beside me and in a couple of hours everything will disappear into total darkness. I don't want anyone's misplaced passion for pity. I don't want consolation. I don't want a hug. I can't even imagine wanting to have sex ever again. I want to try and imagine the future knowing that this is the beginning of the end, that there is no turning back. The doctor told me that I have to come back to the hospital next week for more tests. Perhaps I'll make it. Perhaps this is only the beginning, the beginning of the end of the emptiness I have always carried around within me.

The Question

Rob Walker

"Isn't it interesting that we haven't really changed the ageing process despite all our tinkering? Now that I'm 40, I've noticed that my body shape has begun to subtly change. Despite all of our modern dietary limitations, exercise regimes, nanobot and reconstructive surgery, I'm still developing the ancient cliché *middle-age spread*. Or *growing gut* as my insubordinate adolescent offspring refer to it."

Milton re-read his first paragraph. It wasn't a bad start. The kind of thing his "readers" (listeners really) had come to expect. Self-deprecating, a dig at the teenage children, not too serious. Perhaps he'd change "insubordinate adolescent offspring" — a little pompous and old-fashioned, and many listeners wouldn't know "insubordinate". That was the essence of his current malaise. Perhaps he could rail at the falling education standards once again. And yet he was part of the problem. Here he was, sitting in front of an antique word processor, punching @ antiquated keys to produce "text" which would be recreated as speech by a cyberactor. Speech and vision accessed by millions of Viewer/Listeners over the next few days. Most of these VLs were highly intelligent, but few would be capable of reading the ancient text that Milton used to compose his musings.

It was happening again. His morose mood had re-erected the barrier formerly called *writer's block*. He reread the opening again. No use. Perhaps a short break...

The apartment was dark and silent except for a soft squawk from Mimi the family dodo. Milton usually worked @ nite.

He wandered down to the *kitchen*, the very word one of extreme embarrassment to his children.

"You're a wealthy, successful Muser, Milton!" they'd despair (Never *Dad* — NO one did that anymore.) "Why would you want to prepare your own food?" It was true. He could access any online snack and expect delivery within minutes. By touching "time", "place" and "style" onscreen, he could order anything from 1950 New Orleans Cajun crawfish to 2130 Szechwan Retro-Soyburger — that was part of the cause of his expanding waistline — but sometimes he just enjoyed the novelty of simple food preparation.

The fridge revealed a small piece of Apatosaurus fillet, which he reheated. He could hear his children, thankfully asleep in real time, bemoaning, "Why do you save stuff, Milton? Leftovers are unhygienic and SO twenty-first century. And NOBODY eats dead animal anymore." But Milton still did. He remembered his own father telling him that meat eating was once commonplace, and the excitement of tasting rehabilitated endangered species, and later, the farmed clones of the Formerly Extinct.

FEs were quite the rage for a while, with dinner party menus boasting "Thylacine Ribs in Acacia Seed Sauce" and "Raptor Drumsticks Pan-fried in South Australian Olive Oil". But a number of unfortunate pet Thylacine attacks, not to mention the Tyrannosaur Plains incident, had led to a complete State ban on the cloning or farming of all present and past carnivores. "Another positive example of State Intervention," Milton, who was something of a conservative, had written at the time.

The hoarded cryo-packed apatosaur was quite acceptable in the usual gamy, proto-reptilian way. Milton autorecycled the container and utensil.

There are so many things wrong, Milton pondered. If only the State would intervene more often. The Golden Years, he mused. Perhaps every generation's own adolescence... He should make a note of that for a future piece. The breakdown of many of the corporatised essential services in the mid-first century had led to massive nationalisation and ultimately State Intervention by century's end. Great times... The State really caring for its people, Localization undoing many of the excesses of Millennial Globalization... Yet now, the 'Laissez-Fairies' were fighting back. Didn't people learn anything from History?

Trouble was, they didn't. Nobody taught history. Or read it. Nobody read. If it wasn't available as a 5sec vidbyte, no-one was interested...

The morbid depression was coming back again. He must fight it. His days as a Philosopher were over. Non-vocational tertiary teaching was as dead as the tyrannosaur. He was a Muser, now. Highly paid to amuse, entertain, divert. He'd make an appointment with the therapist again tomorrow. Milton washed down a fluoxetine with a 2099 McLaren Vale Petit Verdot.

*　*　*

It was more than the gut. That could be fixed with a few Surgery-implanted lipo-scavenger nanobots. He wouldn't even need to take the day off. Follicle regeneration would take care of the thinning patch @ his crown. And with hormone replacement and a few more artificial yottabytes to augment his memory, there was no conceivable reason why he should ever show any of the outward signs of ageing. He was only 0.4 of the way through his life. His income and education had enabled a special privilege — a State-sanctioned child of each gender. He had been taught from earliest memory that he could stay fit and healthy right up to the day of his 100th birthday when he'd be given 10cc of the Final Solution.

Whatever happened to "happy"?

You have everything, Milton, he told himself, staring out-of-focus @ the ancient fridge door. A perfect spouse and offspring... well-paid job... yet there's an emptiness like hunger. He patted his abdomen. It's just the Physical reminders of my own mortality…

He couldn't imagine another 60 empty years of writing jaded humor. He pushed a hidden button under the desk and the tray opened. He drew up 10cc of The Solution into the needle. Looking for the vein in the wrist … a river flowing through a bleak landscape.

* * *

Who was that Second Millennium writer…?

Then, impulsively, he reached for his cyberpad and hit *search. Hamlet.*

Ah yes… *Shakespeare…*

> *"to be*
>
> *or not to be.*
>
> *That is the question…"*

He lay aside the hypodermic on the desk.

Perhaps he'd read the old play just one more time.

Marge

Steven Carr

With her newly purchased blond beehive wig teetering precariously on the top of her graying black hair, Marge attempted in vain to move her head without pushing it further askew. It tilted like the tower in Pisa. Quickly raising her lotion-moistened hands to it as she turned to see what the train schedule on the wall now said, she dug her fingernails painted a glossy crimson red into the fake hair and shifted it back into place, attempting to do so without drawing attention to herself or the plight of her fake hairdo. The train she was waiting on was running late which increased her level of anxiety and made her wish she had put on an extra pair of panties for padding. The wooden train station bench was hard and uncomfortable.

Facing forward once again with the wig balanced above her ears like a frothy yellow multilayered wedding cake, she held her black patent leather clutch in her lap, repeatedly snapping and unsnapping the faux gold catch meant to keep it closed. The sound of the clicking was lost in the din of the station to everyone but Marge, who felt some mild relief at being able to focus on the repetitive action and sound. In the clutch was the remainder of the coins from her son's broken bright pink piggy bank, shattered and raided to finance the taxi ride to the station with a little left over to buy a can of soda in case she had to wait for the train. The can lay unopened on its side resting against her hip, the coolness of it seeping through the thin cotton of her leopard print skintight dress. Her husband Jack had always been partial to wild cats.

·With her legs crossed, and flicking the toe of the gold-colored pump on the foot of the top leg, the entire lower half of Marge's body was kept in constant motion by the foot's movement as if she were sitting on the hood of her clothes washer, producing almost the same effect; coloring her otherwise pale cheeks beneath the peach-colored blush and causing beads of perspiration to form over her upper lip. Since she couldn't see it, she was unaware that the light sweat produced from the combination of being in perpetual motion and the heat of the train station had caused her copper-colored necklace to stain her neck and chest blue-green, giving the appearance she had been choked with a moldy strand of cooked spaghetti.

Unwilling to shake her hair from its perch, she didn't turn her head to see the person who sat down uncomfortably close to her side, pushing the can against her.

"What's a beautiful lady like you doing sitting here all alone?" It was a male voice.

"I'm waiting on my husband," Marge said, increasing the rapidity of clutch snapping and toe flicking.

"He been away on business?" the man asked.

"Something like that," Marge said, keeping her eyes focused on the crowds coming in from and going out to the concourse.

"Is your marriage a happy one?" the man asked.

"Very happy," Marge said.

The man was silent for a moment, then said, "You have a buck so that I can buy myself a can of pop?"

"No, I don't," Marge said. "Please leave me alone."

She felt the man leave her side but didn't hear him as he walked away. A moment later she realized he had stolen her soda.

As a new wave of arriving passengers came in from the concourse the speakers in the station announced that the train her husband was arriving on was also now pulling into the station. To keep her hair balanced, she placed her clutch on the seat, held onto her wig, and stood very slowly. She licked her cherry red lipsticked lips to renew their shine, and walked toward the concourse. Then she remembered her clutch. Turning about abruptly, the beehive toppled down from her head like a toy animal that had lost its stuffing and into her arms raised in spontaneous alarm. She grabbed her clutch from the bench, then frantically, but to no avail, tried to reposition the wig onto her head. Unable to do so, she tucked it under her arm and smoothed back her hair and walked out to the concourse.

Seven years had been a long time to wait for her husband's return. Certainly he would know that she had changed while he had deserted her to live with another woman, Marge considered as she stood on the concourse and watched as the passengers on her husband's train stepped off. Fraught with anticipation and her concern with how she would appear to him after such a long absence, she couldn't hold back the tears, sending rivulets of black mascara down her cheeks.

As the passengers filed past her, and the crowd on the concourse thinned considerably, Marge held her wig to her ample breasts, hoping beyond hope that Jack would get off the train and hadn't abandoned her once again. When he stepped out of the train the first thing she saw him do was stare at another woman's legs.

She walked up to him, opened her clutch and took out a small pistol and shot him in the middle of his forehead.

Waiting

Michael Webb

I am staring at him. We are in his office, his diplomas and
certificates on the wall behind my head. I am sitting, my legs
crossed, waiting. It feels like I have spent my whole life waiting
for men to talk. My father, then boyfriends, my husband, then
bosses, now this cipher of a man. He's slightly rumpled, the
sexy, casual look, balding on top, neatly trimmed beard, brown
eyes. He looks like a professor, an intelligent, gentle face that
will probably edge into sloppy fat as he gets even older. He is
sitting behind a desk next to the door. Along the wall to my left
is a bookcase holding a number of leather binders. An air
cleaner purrs on the floor

I feel wrung out. I have been talking for ten minutes, going
over and over the same territory with him, rocketing from tears
back to silence while he just sits there, impassive, a stone
immune to erosion. I want to scream, to cry again, to bash my
skull against the wall, to somehow evoke an emotion from him,
something to replace this empty and sterile silence. I think of all
the confessions this room has heard, the abortions, the homo-
sexual dalliances, the betrayals of home and hearth and soul.

The fishtank in the corner gurgles as the filter turns on. I
watch the oxygen bubbling through the water.

"After all that," he'd said finally, his voice soft, "what is it
you want? What can you do now? What is it that makes you
happy?" I heard the question, and I understood it perfectly

133

well, but it was constructed of concepts I couldn't grasp. The idea of existing for myself, of filling a role other than one of service to others, was as foreign as suddenly becoming an acrobat. I knew what he was asking, but I had no idea how to answer, and suddenly I was the one to fall silent.

Happy Numbers

DS Levy

"So tell me again. When is Abby's piano recital?" He palms the paper cup back and forth between his hands.

They're in the bookstore café. Large posters of writers–Emerson, Woolf, Hemingway–eye them from above.

Across the table, she stares at her nails. Her burgundy polish is chipped off. He looks at his own–lined with black dirt.

"I'll try to be there," he says. "I'll sure as hell try."

She sips Oolong tea with honey. The paper tab on the tea bag is wet and drips on the table. She soaks up the pool with a napkin.

"It's not for me," she says. "For her."

"I know that. Look, we'll figure this out. It's not like we're the first couple who's ever had to do this."

"Twenty-ninth. Of October. The recital's in the gym, not the auditorium."

"Yeah, the auditorium–"

"No! The gym. They're having it in the gym. Because–" She shrugs, clicking her nails on the table. "I don't know why. A mix-up in the schedule."

He sips his coffee, runs his thumb over the plastic lid.

"So, Halloween? You going to take her trick-or-treating, or am I?"

She sits back in her chair. "This is what I'm talking about."

135

He looks up. Her eyes are tearing. "C'mon," he whispers, reaching out and touching her lightly on her wrist, but she pulls back.

"Last year we all went out. All three of us," she says, wiping a tear off her cheek. "Her first time. Remember how it rained, but she didn't care? She loved it."

He smiles, sips his coffee.

"One of us is always going to lose. This, what we're doing. It's a losing proposition."

He says, "If we had a calendar it might make this easier."

"Jesus! Listen to yourself! '*Make this easier?*" This isn't one of your *projects*, you know."

"Look, I'm trying here, okay? You know what the judge said. Keeping our lines of communication open."

"Next thing you know we'll be creating one of those—one of those things you use at work, those project management time line thingies."

He furrows his brow, looks out across the bookstore, toward the aisles and then over at the magazine racks. He's not sure what she's talking about—and what does his job have to do with anything?

"You know," she chimes, "that chart with lines for each step of the project? The ones that overlap?"

"What? A Gantt Chart?"

"Yes, *that*. A Gantt Chart. But our 'steps' are going to overlap for the rest of our lives. And truthfully? Sometimes I don't even want to look at you again, I can't stand the sight of you."

Rivulets of tears stream down her cheeks. He slumps back in his chair. A Broadway show tune, one of those up-tempo happy numbers she always loves, blares out of the café's speakers. He hates those songs.

"Look at us," she sniffles.

He stands up and walks over to the calendars section, grabbing the first one he sees, then takes it back to the table. When he sits down, he realizes there's nothing to write with.

"You don't have a pen, do you?" he asks her.

She shakes her head.

He swaggers over to the girl behind the counter and asks if he can borrow a pen. She smiles and hands him one. He smiles back. She's young enough to be his daughter, has gorgeous long silky red hair.

"Promise I'll bring it right back," he tells her with a wink. He hesitates, tapping his nails on the counter, then returns to the table. He sits down and tears off the shrink-wrapping, flips to October. The ink pen is dry and he has to scratch several times before he can circle the twenty-ninth.

"Okay," he says. "That's a start."

They hunch over the calendar, circling dates, arguing quietly. The café worker's shift ends and another girl stands behind the counter. Two hours later, they've mapped out the rest of the year. Each page of the glossy calendar features a different adorable puppy, but neither one has noticed.

Bliss of Contentment

Tom Fegan

Friday night's black curtain draped over the city of Dallas, Texas as luminous streetlights blazed pathways for the night world's inhabitants. Traffic lights controlled the cars loaded with revelers, while neon signs posed as a beacon for their destinations ready for business. Mockingbird Lane offered a thoroughfare of action accented by passenger jets that roared in and out of Love Field. I encountered those who played in darkness as the counter man at Bo's 24 Cafe near the airport. This crowd would drift in and out with Friday and Saturday being the heaviest traffic days at the cafe. Hookers, exotic dancers, pimps, cops, security guards, night janitors and patrons seeking good times by touring the neighboring watering holes ended up at the cafe during my shift.

The shift drudgery lifted when Ray Cain, a middle-aged bachelor podiatrist entered in the wee hours of each Saturday morning to disclose his barhopping activities to me which shattered the monotony. I was always happy to see him. He used the Doctor title to woo women keeping his specialization secret and fermenting in their minds that he was a physician. He drank only ginger ale to gain advantage of his targets and keep a clear head. His prowl started no earlier than midnight. "By then," he joked, "I'm fresh and look great to the women who have been hit on and pawed at by other drunks." He maintained a well-groomed appearance accented by a stylish suit and tie. His thick mane of silver hair offered a mature and successful look for his targets.

This tale would be different. I poured his coffee, which he took black, and transcended into his personal audience. He sipped his coffee and expounded on his adventure. "I met a goddess," he beamed, "a Venus in spiked heels!" He continued to verbally sketch her: tall and slinky with a full head of blonde hair that flowed past her shoulders.

"Her emerald eyes were bright as any star." He licked his lips. His sensual description of the woman's streamlined physique was profiled by a dark evening dress. A shapely and muscular leg was exposed from the slit that began from the hip. A low cut front accented supple breasts. Her hips firmly rounded. A long cigarette holder situated between two fingers. She dragged in and exhaled tobacco-laden mist out with her neck craned toward the heavens. As she slung a small jacket over one shoulder, her eyes met Ray's. The podiatrist was mesmerized by her erotic aura, encircling her and enticing him.

"She was a working girl too," he mused.

I became curious. "That good looking she's gotta be a cop," I surmised.

My bluntness shocked him.

Ray frowned, "Well, she got my two hundred dollars."

Dr. Goldberg's Full Moon

Joanne Jagoda

Pull me over to the window. I want to see the moon. It's a silvery, luminescent wonder. Just like the night I met my Emma. Come on sonny. Take me there.

Where does the old man want me to push him? He's grunting and pointing with his bony finger. "Mr. Goldberg, what do you want? You got to take a crap? You're pointing somewhere, I get that. Hey, now don't try to get up yourself. Sit down and don't get all riled up. You want me to wheel you somewhere? You got to go to the bathroom? Ya' want some water?"

Oy, this kid is dense. The window. The window. I want to look out the window, the one that leads to the rose garden. I want to see the full moon.

"Wish I could read your mind, old man. That stroke was a bitch to leave you without your words. My *abuela* had a stroke, and I know it's frustrating for you."

I don't need you to feel sorry for me. I just want to move to the window. Oh, good there's Bernie. She'll know what to do.

"Hey, Bernie, old man Goldberg is agitated. He wants something but I sure as hell don't know what it is. You've taken care of him, haven't you? Maybe you know what he is trying to say."

"Derrick, first of all show a little respect. It is not Mr. Goldberg. It is Dr. Goldberg. He was an orthopedic surgeon.

140

Very well respected in his field. His wife Emma told me all about him. She came in every day and took him to the café, or out to the rose garden. They were a sweet couple but after his second stroke it was really tough. He couldn't speak and was belligerent. Then they found out she had pancreatic cancer and she didn't last long. Dr. Goldberg is a lost soul. He waits for her every day."

"Oh well, shit. How was I supposed to know he was somebody back in the day. He's just a blubbering mess now as far as I can see. I shouldn't have said that. Now don't report me."

Dr. Goldberg was keenly listening. He could understand everything and wanted to kiss Bernie for her kind words.

"Derrick, I'll sit with Dr. Goldberg. I'm off in a half hour but I don't mind staying a little longer. Maybe I can figure out what he wants. And I won't report you this time, but you'd best watch that smart mouth of yours. We respect all our patients here at the Home whether they can talk or not talk, wear diapers or just sit around drooling all day. You get it?"

"Yeah, yeah. Uh, Dr. Goldberg, Bernie here is going to take over for me. She is going to figure out why you are unhappy."

"Good evening sir. How are you tonight? Did you like the meatloaf for dinner? Tomorrow is fresh turkey. It should be yummy. Now, now don't you cry. I'm here for you."

Bernie, just take me to the window. I want to see the moon.

"Dr. Goldberg you are gesturing. I got it! You want to go out to the rose garden. It's too cold to do that now, but I could take you to the window in the back and you can sit there to your heart's content. Yes, that's it. You're smiling. Hang on, we're going for a ride. Yes, I've got you in a good spot. You can see outside and enjoy that beautiful full moon. Is it the moon you want to see? Oh yes I bet it is. Did you and Emma fall in love on a night like this? Now don't cry. I'll go and get you a

141

cup of mint tea and some of those butter cookies you like and let you rest here a spell. I'll be back in twenty minutes."

Thank you thank you Bernie. Now go on and leave me in peace. Now I'm happy.

Dear Emma, do you remember? It was a night like this, crisp and cold... April, 1943 just before I was shipped out. Darling, we met at that dance for servicemen at St. Dominic's in North Beach. You were serving the punch. O Lord, you were prettiest of all the girls. You had on a light blue cashmere cardigan, with the first button open. It matched your eyes. I never saw a girl like you with your bouncy brown curls. You wouldn't dance with me at first. I didn't give up and finally we danced to Glenn Miller, In the Mood. I was a good dancer and from that moment you were mine. The other soldiers wanted to cut in but I didn't let them. I wanted that dance to last forever.

You let me take you home. Your house was on Beach St. When the cab dropped us, we didn't want to let the night end. We started walking and ended up at a pier near the wharf. The sea lions were barking and the fog was rolling in. It was chilly. You let me put my arm around you because your teeth were chattering. Suddenly the fog cleared and the full moon was over us like a magical goddess blessing us with her luminescent glory. I kissed you and asked you to wait for me until I returned from the service. We didn't see each other for two years but you wrote me letters every day. Thinking of you kept me alive when I was on the battlefield stitching up those poor boys and putting together their broken bones.

Oh Emma. I miss you so. Hang on dear. I'm coming to you. We'll dance again to Glenn Miller. We'll kiss under the light of the moon."

"Dr. Goldberg? Dr. Goldberg? I've got your tea and cookies. Oh no. Dr. Goldberg. Someone come to help me! Dr. Goldberg has... well, I expect he's gone to his dear Emma."

Cargo Pants

Elizabeth Bruce

One dollar. One dollar. OK, OK, that's all I need, Davey thought, his 11-year-old brain scrambling to make this new problem not a problem, not an emergency, not another humiliating mistake he had to call his mom about and how would he do that anyway without any money?

He could handle this. He'd found his way to the Metro station, hadn't he, even when the bus driver wouldn't let him on.

"Sorry kid," the driver had said, "It's my first day on the job, so I've gotta follow the rules. Your monthly pass expired yesterday, buddy. I can't let you on. Sorry."

Sure, Davey'd been scared at first, this had never happened before, then he was pissed at his mom for not remembering to get him a new pass—she was usually on top of stuff like that—but then, he'd remembered that he knew the way, at least the way the bus went from his school to the Metro, so he could just follow the route, and that's what he'd done. Walked the bus route all the way even though it was kinda cold outside, and now here he was, safe at the Metro. Was that cool or what? Alright! He was one smart kid. Yeah OK, he was late, his mom would be pissed, but he was late a lot and she always got over it, and besides, wasn't it kind of her fault anyway?

But, now, crap, he'd even lost his stupid dollar, the one he hadn't spent on lunch the way he was supposed to, the one he was gonna use to buy a jumbo Reese's Peanut Butter Cup instead, but now, GA-A-A-A, even that was gone and how the hell was he going to buy a Metro ticket?

Again, he searched his pockets, the ones in back without the holes and the ones in front with the holes that he'd forgotten about—again—that had loosed his dollar into the world—again. Stupid pants, he thought, why'd they have to have holes in them, why hadn't he asked his mom to fix them and didn't she check his pockets all the time anyway so why hadn't she seen the holes and fixed them already?

"One dollar," Davey said aloud this time, loud enough for the people crowding around the farecard machine to hear. "One dollar, one dollar," he repeated, pulling his empty pockets inside out this time but all he found were the stupid pebbles they'd been throwing on top of the sports shed at school before the security guard caught them and made them stop. "Don't make me have to tell Mr. Pope, now, boys," she had said. "You knuckleheads stop this nonsense now, you hear?"

Come on, come on, Davey thought, his stomach starting to clench up, there's gotta be a dollar somewhere in one of these stupid pockets.

The line in front of the farecard machine was growing longer. An old lady in a blue coat looked down at him. She had that look his mother had when he pretended to be asleep but really was just faking it so he could skip social studies class first period with Miz what's her name, who made them copy the entire glossary from the back of the book like it was real learning and not just some stupid busy work even his dad thought was crap.

"One dollar," he said again under his breath, peeking at the lady in the blue coat from behind his shaggy white boy hair. This time he checked the side pockets of his cargo pants, the

144

ones that hung low beneath his knees, too big for his small frame his mom said, bigger than he was they were. "What you gonna hide in there, buddy, a bottle of vodka or just a few Molotov cocktails?" she had asked, sarcastic like she always was. He didn't know what a Molotov cocktail was but he sure as hell wasn't gonna let his mother know that, not her who was against this plan all along: against him taking the subway home alone all across town every day without so much as a beeper to keep in touch.

"One dollar, one dollar, one dollar, one dollar, one dollar," he muttered, his words echoing in his chest, once for each pocket, once for each month before his 12th birthday, once for each time he'd promised his mom he'd come right home after school.

"One dollar," came a final echo. The boy looked up. The lady in the blue coat was still staring at him, a crisp dollar bill in her hand.

"Looks like you could use this, young man," she said and smiled that same grandma smile his neighbor had when she caught him up top the tallest tree on the block, the same smile his mom would have, he was sure, after he told her what all had happened, the same smile his heart was having right now looking up at this nice lady.

"Oh, yes ma'am," he said even though he never said "ma'am." Oh man, where did that come from, he thought, and suddenly, before he could stop it, before he could get his game face on, that little-kid-happy-grin he hated so much, that old ladies and especially his mom liked so much burst across his face.

"Yes, ma'am," he said again and so help him he didn't even care this time if he sounded like a dork, "One dollar's all I need."

Summer Daze

Meryl Baer

The old woman's chest rose and fell in sync with the ocean water lapping her feet. Lost in the salty smells and sounds of the sea, sprawled in a beach chair inches off the sand, head stretched back, straw hat covering her face, she lounged the day away.

The sun beat down on her glistening body. Wrinkled hands speckled with spots darker than her tan rested on her round stomach. Bare legs stretched out, pedicured toes curled into the sand, low waves rolled closer as the tide swept in.

Parents berated screaming kids to stay close, a lifeguard's whistle beckoned swimmers to shore. Shrill voices pierced the air. Sunbathers and sand castle builders kept up a steady chatter.

The old woman remained oblivious. A breeze chilled her arms and a smile crossed her lips. She pictured the multi-colored green, red and yellow mohair sweater Mom knit one year for the first day of school. Was it fourth grade? Fifth? Maybe seventh? The sweater found an honored place in her closet for decades. One day she carefully placed it in a bag destined for Goodwill, hoping someone would fall in love with it and wear it once more.

She could hear music. *Mamma Mia.* We haven't gotten together for a *Mamma Mia* night in a long time, she thought. Must get the girls together again, maybe on my birthday.

A swishing sound passed her head and something smacked into her stomach. She stirred, unsure where she was and what was happening. Rubbing her stomach and grimacing, she opened her eyes and shielding her face from the sun, noticed a man step in front of her. She clutched the ball and patted her stomach. She was OK, just startled. The rubber ball appeared small and harmless.

"I'm so sorry. My daughter," and the man pointed to a toddler about three years old, "threw the ball."

"I'm fine, a little sore. I understand. I have kids and grandkids…" What were they doing now? Besides having babies. She barely remembered when *she* had babies.

She stood, brushed sand off her legs and looked at the sky. The sun had sunk along the horizon. Umbrella shadows stretched across the sand. Most people had already left the beach.

Time to go.

Turning her back to the sea the old woman folded her chair and grabbed the strap, snatched her sandals and began plodding away, dragging the chair across the sand.

Death Breath

Mark Govier

"Wow!"

My brother starts first.

Then I go "Wow!" just to keep up.

Here we are, our whole small family, minus my mother, standing in front of the Death Monitors, in the Death Section, of the Aged Care Facility. We're all feeling happy, sort of. We're here to watch our Grandad die. He's 98, so we've been told. Not that I or my brother really know. Well, he definitely looks really, really old.

My mother's never liked her father-in-law, called him a decomposing bag of offal, for ages, even in front of Dad. Not that I know why, really. But Grandad's definitely not well.

My brother and I were told his wife, Dad's mother, my other grandmother, was put into another Elite branch a couple of years ago. My brother and I haven't seen her since. Neither has my mother, or father, or so they say. She went senile, so they said, couldn't even recognise herself.

"They'll keep her alive there until at least 100," my mother sometimes says, unhappily, as they're paying, this is to my father when they think I'm out of hearing.

Bang! The Death Monitor hots up. We all hear Grandad, wheezing. Mum and Dad told us they paid a lot so Grandad wouldn't die in a General Death Ward. Dad says there's hundreds of very old people in these, all lined up, dying one by one, wheezing away in their beds. Dad says the smell in General is incredible, despite all the deodorant that's pumped in. Dad says he knows all this because he's been with friends to visit theirs. He said it made him throw up.

My brother and I think Grandad's pretty lucky to be in one of these Special Facilities Rooms. This is not because Mum and Dad are generous. Mum and Dad said they sold the rights to his death to a show called *Death Breath*. Dad says it's a popular show, but it's Y Certificate, which means it's Real Adults Only, which my brother and I can't watch. Not even on the Darkest Web. But here we are watching the live death of a relative, like now, because he's a relative. Now that's real logic!

"Look at that," says Dad, pointing, "see, they're switching to Inner Sight."

My brother and I know all that, not that we say. Instead we humour Dad.

"It's a special device fitted into the dying person's brain," says Dad.

My brother and I continue to pretend to be amazed.

We wink at each other, mockingly. Thankfully Dad doesn't see.

Now the screen's a blur. It's what Grandad sees. There's the Death Room, all faint pastel green paint. There are two Death Nurses, dressed in faint paste green. More blur. Whorls stream in. Grandad's looking at the lights above. A gurgle. Another gurgle. The face of one of the Death Nurses fills the screen. Blur.

The Death Nurse asks, "What did you say Mr Sith?"

No response.

"He's ready to go," says this Death Nurse, to the other one. Blackness.

"Has he died?" I ask Dad, beginning to feel really bored. I start to pick my favourite pimple.

149

"Shhh," says Dad, "just watch."

Dad's obviously seen plenty of episodes of *Death Breath*.

Still blackness. I'm getting totally restless. A loud gurgling. Silence. A faint light.

"Here we go," says Dad.

A stream of exploding, patterned light.

"Wow," say my brother and I. We're still pretending, a bit.

Another loud gurgle, then a loud sigh.

"He's almost gone," says Dad, "now watch this."

Slowly, a distant spiral of patterns and light appears. It veers closer. Explodes. It's pretty bright. Quite impressive, sort of. Then it's back to blackness.

"I thought it would be better than that," I say to Dad as the hospital doors silently whoosh closed behind us.

"It is usually," says Dad leading us across the hospital car park.

"The problem with Grandad was he was 9/10 dead anyway, and that was a year ago…"

My brother and I start whinging for ice cream.

"Come on Dad," we say together, "we really, really need something after all that!"

We smile extra hard, and Dad tells Fred, his new self-driving car, to go to the nearest ice cream shop. Victory!

"Here we are," he says, as Fred pulls up outside a nearby Ice Head shop.

Now my brother and I are really happy.

"Wow," we say together, "wow, wow and triple wow…"

Constant Praise

Catherine McLeod

I look up at her, slightly bent over the kitchen sink. I watch as she picks up the gloves, methodically pulls the rubber up each forearm, pokes each finger into place and finishes with a slight wiggle, a flex of the palms.

The water gushes from the tap in a steady stream. Soon the foam is visible over the metal rim, the steam rising up to meet her face. She brushes hair from her eyes with an elbow, gloved hands already covered in soap. Submerged in the hot suds, they scrub and scour and wipe the plates clean. There is a sureness in the actions, a certainty I dream of, even without the opposable thumbs.

"What is my purpose?" I ask her.

She turns to reply. Smiles down at me. I already know she has not understood.

"Good boy."

Lovelandtown Tavern

Matt DeVirgiliis

The Lovelandtown lift bridge lurched and stuck in place, the roadway stalled twenty feet above the street.

A man appeared, his orange reflector vest shining as the bridge's red and yellow lights blinked on and off. He pulled his wool cap on over his ears and spoke into a little black box, his breath a puff of smoke. Few cars idled behind the warning arms on either side.

One car, a Mercedes, pulled into the lot of the Lovelandtown Tavern, nestled by the bridge on the west side.

The dark bar forced your eyes to adjust. If you were lucky enough to have a companion, you could read their emotions but not see their flaws. Locals frequented, mostly roughneck types – fishermen, mechanics, lifelong waitresses from other establishments. Smoking had been banned years ago, but a lingering haze remained. You spent your night with mostly old-timers and those worn out from life, the salt of the earth. You left smelling like stale beer and black licorice but feeling wholesome.

James Hubert III sat at the bar. It was late. His wife and kids were long in bed and he knew he should be, too. But with the Lovelandtown lift bridge stuck in mid-air, a drink beckoned him. He sat next to Vince DeSantos, a small, stout man, with a bowling ball head and dry, cracked knuckles. Vince humphed when he walked. James and Vince grew up together.

"Really like this place," said Vince.

"Me too," said James. "We probably know everyone in here."

"Me more than you," said Vince.

"But they leave us to our Rolling Rock."

Vince rolled his thermal sleeves to his elbows and drooped his shoulders as he ran his thumbs under his Carhartt coverall straps. "Things keep me warm on the job," he said, "but make me sweat my ass off inside." He tilted his green beer bottle and gulped as he drank. James drank, too.

"This beer brings me back," said James. He rolled up his dress shirtsleeves and tucked the cufflinks into his breast pocket. Both men leaned their forearms on the bar, their Rolling Rock bottles standing at attention before them.

"Brings you back from what?" asked Vince. "You only live over the bridge."

James held up the green bottle and peered through it like a looking glass. He stuck his nose on the opening and sniffed.

"Remember when we'd help my dad with yard work during the summer?" said James. "We'd help him cut the lawn and weed whack as he ran around and trimmed the trees and reposted the fence. Like teenage boys are supposed to do, he'd say. Then we'd break and sit on the back step and he'd crack one of these. It was the only time he drank beer. He'd take a sip and then pass it to us and say, one sip each. Nothing better than the smell of freshly mowed grass and the twang of this beer. The best days I can remember," said James.

"Were they, though?"

James peered out the window and watched the men on the bridge scurry like mice trying to find their cheese. "I was happy," James said.

"It was different, then," said Vince. "I have Desiree and little Vinny now. I worry now."

"My Jimmy fell off his scooter and split his forehead last week," said James. "Sheryl called me and my throat locked up. He's fine, she said, he's got a few stitches and a lot of blood, but the head bleeds. I wanted to run home and hug him. But I couldn't leave. Even if I did, I probably couldn't have found a flight home at that time."

"But you have it all," said Vince. "You parked your Mercedes next to a twenty-year-old pickup truck. You have a house with a bay view and another with a mountain view."

"That's not what warms me up, though, Vin. It could all go away. At least you enjoy what you do. Every day. And you're home to enjoy the important things."

"What would it have been?"

"Archeology," said James.

"There's no money in that."

"That's what my parents said. But there's learning and digging and exploring. No cubicles. No business class."

"Don't wish away everything you've got," said Vince.

The yellow and red flashing lights stopped flickering through the tavern windows and the bar fell quiet. James turned to see workmen on the bridge climbing into their trucks. He stuck twenty dollars on the bar. "This one's on me," he said.

"I'll get the next one," said Vince.

They stood, shook hands, and hugged, slapping each other on the back. "Come see us sometime," said James, gripping Vince tightly as if not wanting to let go.

"I will," said Vince. "I work Saturdays and some Sundays. I'll have to get over the bridge to you. Tell Sheryl we say hello."

"Ride?"

"Nah, the fresh air is good for me," said Vince.

They walked outside. James climbed into his coupe. He watched Vince stuff his hands into his pockets and bury his chin into his coveralls and walk west, disappearing into the cold night.

James Hubert pulled out of the parking lot and sped up the bridge, his Mercedes' lights fading as he passed over the top and down the other side.

A Happy Family

Wayne Scheer

So I said to Ellie, I said, "When pigs fly, that's when I'll apologize." And she said, "Yeah, and monkeys'll fly out your ass when I accept."

We had just been kidding around, making fun of our families. I had this senile aunt who would sit in front of the TV with the set off and watch the Brooklyn Dodgers. This was long after they had moved to Los Angeles.

"Did you see that throw Furillo made from right field?" she'd ask.

"Sure, Aunt Sophie. I saw that. Great arm."

That led to how Ellie thought we need a bigger TV and when I said, "We should wait'll this one breaks down to replace it," she called me cheap like my father.

So I said something about how Ellie is like her mother, especially with the new haircut she got.

"You damn well better apologize for that crack," she said. "Or you'll be sleeping on the couch."

And that's when pigs and monkeys started flying, and she slammed the bedroom door so hard Claire woke up crying.

So I went to her. "Everything's okay, baby. Me and Mommy, we're just letting off some steam is all. We're just playing, like you do with your friends sometimes."

Then, before I could even kiss Claire good night, Ellie came in and pushed me away like I got head lice or something, and she sat down on the bed next to Claire.

"It's all right, honey, Mommy's here."

"Yeah," I said. "Mommy and Daddy are both here."

Claire stopped crying and I saw how cute she looked in her little pink bunny pajamas. I also saw that Ellie was wearing this short nightgown, and it was riding up her legs as she rocked Claire.

It's hard staying mad when your daughter looks so damn cute and your wife's flashing pubes.

So I said, "I'm sorry." I looked at Ellie and now she and Claire were crying. "I love both of you."

"And you don't really look like your mother," I assured her.

"Yes, I do. It's this stupid haircut."

She held out her hand and I took it.

"Pigs don't really fly, do they?" Claire asks. "And monkeys won't come out of Daddy's—"

"No," I said.

And we laughed like one happy family.

Selective Learning

Paul Beckman

The moose with the re-usable shopping bag filled with magazines hanging from his large antlers rang the front doorbell again. He is unique with his crooked moose smile and appears happy and a little cute and all but if he could learn to do all that he could learn to read my 'No Solicitors' signs that are posted prominently around my picket-fenced half acre lot tucked in the woods at the end of a cul-de-sac.

After School

Gwendolyn Joyce Mintz

Megan's the first girl in class to get boobs. We are not happy. We hate her for that now; not just because she thinks she knows everything. But maybe they've made her dumb 'cause most every day our teacher, Mr. Max, keeps her after school.

Authors

Meryl Baer

lives at the New Jersey shore. She is blessed with numerous relatives and friends who make their way to her door at the shore during the summer. No one visits in winter, so she writes. Her work has appeared in anthologies (most recently *Angel Bumps*), websites (eg. *GRAND Magazine*, *Midlife Blvd.*, *TheNewVerse.News*), and she is a National Society of Newspaper Columnists award winner. Check out more of her work at her blog: http://sixdecadesandcounting.blogspot.com.

Judy Shepps Battle

has been writing essays and poems long before retiring from being a psychotherapist and sociology professor. She is a New Jersey resident, addictions specialist, consultant and freelance writer. Her poems have been accepted in a variety of publications including *Ascent Aspirations*, *Battered Suitcase*, *Caper Literary Journal*, *Poetry Magazine*, *Raleigh Review*, *The Tishman Review*, and *Wilderness House Literary Review*.

Paul Beckman

was one of the winners in the 2016 Best Small Fictions with his story *Healing Time*. His stories are widely published in print and online and in the following magazines amongst others: *Connecticut Review*, *Raleigh Review*, *Litro*, *Playboy*, and *Thrice Fiction*. Paul lives in Connecticut and earned his MFA from Bennington College. He hosts the FBomb NY flash fiction reading series monthly at KGB in New York. Find his published story website at www.paulbeckmanstories.com, and his blog at www.pincusb.com.

Robert Beveridge

makes noise at xterminal.bandcamp.com and writes poetry just outside Cleveland, OH. Recent appearances in *Chiron Review*, *Riverrun*, and *Third Wednesday*, among others.

Claudia Bierschenk

is a translator and writer. Her works has been published with *Pure Slush*, *SAND Magazine*, *Alligator Stew*, Pig Ear Press, Tangerine Press, among others. She lives in Berlin with her son.

Arthur Black

learned to read at the age of four. His father bought books at estate sales, had them shipped home, and encouraged him to read as many as possible. Born in Brooklyn, N.Y., he won his first writing award as a sophomore in Brooklyn's famous Erasmus Hall High School, and he has continued to write fiction ever since, even during his award-winning career as an advertising agency creative director.

Rick Blum

has been chronicling life's vagaries for more than 25 years as a nightclub owner, high-tech manager, market research mogul, and old geezer. His poems and essays have appeared in *Humor Times*, *Boston Literary Magazine*, and *The Satirist*, among others. Currently, he is holed up in his office trying to pen the perfect bio, which he plans to share as soon as he stops laughing at the sheer futility of this effort.

J. Bradley

is the author of the flash fiction collection *Neil & Other Stories* forthcoming from Whiskey Tit Books in 2018. He lives at jbradleywrites.com.

Elizabeth Bruce

is a writer/actor/educator, originally from Texas and now based in Washington D.C. Her novel *And Silent Left the Place* won Washington Writers' Publishing House's Award, with distinctions from *ForeWord Magazine* and Texas Institute of Letters. She has been published in the USA, UK, and Australia in publications including *FireWords Quarterly*, *Pure Slush*, *Inklette* and others and anthologies by *Vine Leaves Literary Journal*, Weasel and Gargoyle Presses. Her newest book is CentroNia's *Theatrical Journey Playbook: Introducing Science to Early Learners through Guided Pretend Play*. She has had fellowships at DCCAH and McCarthey Dressman Education Foundation.

Irene Buckler

taught in Australian primary schools for three decades, during which time she wrote many educational programs, stories for children, and poetry, which have appeared in publications for children in the United Kingdom and in Australia. A flash fiction finalist in 2017's Hysteria (UK) and Field of Words, Irene writes mainly about people, finding exploring human behaviour to be an endless source of inspiration.

Colin W. Campbell

writes short fiction and poetry in Sarawak on the tropical green island of Borneo and far away in Yunnan in southwest China. Find more at www.colincampbell.org.

Don Kingfisher Campbell

MFA from AULA, has taught at Occidental College for 33 years, been a coach and judge for Poetry Out Loud, a performing poet/teacher for Red Hen Press Youth Writing Workshops, L.A. Coordinator and Board Member of CPITS, poetry editor of the *Angel City Review*, publisher of *Spectrum* magazine, and host of the Saturday Afternoon Poetry reading series in Pasadena, California. For awards, features, and publication credits, please go to http://dkc1031.blogspot.com.

Steven Carr

lives in Richmond, Va. and began his writing career as a military journalist. He has had over a hundred short stories published internationally in print and online magazines, literary journals and anthologies. His plays have been produced in several U.S. states. He was a 2017 Pushcart Prize nominee. He is on Twitter @carrsteven960 and on Facebook at https://www.facebook.com/profile.php?id=100012966314127.

Kersten Christianson

is a raven-watching, moon-gazing Alaskan. When not exploring the summer lands and dark winter of the Yukon, she lives in Sitka, Alaska. She holds an MFA in Creative Writing (University of Alaska Anchorage) and recently published her first collection of poetry *Something Yet to Be Named* (Aldrich Press, 2017). Find more at www.kerstenchristianson.com.

Martin Christmas

has an M.A. in Australian Cultural Studies. He has been published in Australian print literary journals, including *Friendly Street Poets* readers (SA), *Pure Slush* (SA), *Tamba* (NSW) and overseas online journals including *Illya's Honey*, *Red River Review* (USA), and *StepAway Magazine* (UK). He teaches presentation elements to young poets. His chapbook poetry collection, *Immediate Reflections*, was published in 2016 and his second chapbook, *The Deeper Inner*, in 2017 (both Gininderra Press).

Jan Chronister

lives and writes in the woods near Maple, Wisconsin. She doesn't write when she's happy or about happy things, so this theme was a stretch.

Judah Eli Cricelli

was born in Adelaide, South Australia. His first 19 years of life have been a series of far-too-fortunate events leaving him wondering when fate, or rather, debilitating physical illness, will catch up with him. When not embarrassing himself and bringing shame to his family, Judah likes to fritter away his spare time by consuming packet after packet of Nissin Food Holdings ® Demae Brand Ramen. He also writes poems.

Ruth Z. Deming

has had her work published in lit mags including *Mad Swirl*, *Literary Yard*, *Creative Nonfiction* and *River Poets*. She is part of 'The

Beehive', an every Saturday writers' group that gives gentle feedback to one another. She lives in Willow Grove, a suburb of Philadelphia. She is the founder and director of New Directions, a support group that helps people with depression and bipolar disorder, and their loved ones. View their website at www.newdirectionsupport.org, and view Ruth's blog at www.ruthzdeming.blogspot.com. As always, she is delighted to be part of *Pure Slush*.

Matt Devirgiliis

lives with his wife and two daughters – his inspiration – in the small beach town of Point Pleasant, New Jersey. His fiction has been published by Pure Slush Books and Truth Serum Press, and at *52/250 – A Year in Flash*, and *Istanbul Literary Review*. Prior to fiction, he wrote and produced television shows for The Discovery Channel, TLC, HGTV, and Baby First Television. Read more of his work at mattdevir.wordpress.com.

Tom Fegan

was born and raised in Fort Worth, Texas. At age 12 he began working in his family's downtown restaurant Burger & Shake. After college and several years in the steel industry, Tom now works as a security professional. He is contentedly divorced and is pursuing a writing career.

Nod Ghosh

has had work feature in various New Zealand and international publications. Find further details about her work at her website: http://www.nodghosh.com/about/. 'Mokopuna' is written for Bo Violet, a very smart young woman, whose beauty lies in her kindness and sense of fun.

Walter Giersbach

moves between genres, from mystery to humor, speculative fiction to romance with a little non-fiction for good measure. His work has appeared in print and online in over two dozen publications. He's also bounced from Fortune 500 firms to university posts, and homes in eight states and a couple of Asian countries. He now lives in New Jersey, a nice place to visit, but he doesn't want to die there.

Mark Govier

grew up in Adelaide ... fiction, *Trials of Nian Gao* set in future China, out now... Published playwright, *Dead Virgins*, about art, drugs & crime... Poetry, *Cemetery Life*, about working in a crematorium, accepted for publication in the UK... Flash fiction, stories published in *Pure Slush* and elsewhere... Spent 20 years travelling... 100 countries...

Andrew Grenfell

lives in Brisbane, Australia, in a house on the edge of a patch of forest. He likes to write, and read, of course. He works as a mathematician and software developer: not necessarily easy mining for story-telling. That's why he also travels all over the world. He wishes everyone was kinder to each other and doesn't understand why people don't read books instead of Facebooking on their phones.

John Grey

is a Brisbane, Australia-born poet, US resident. Recently published in *Examined Life Journal, Studio One, Columbia Review*; work coming in *Leading Edge, Poetry East* and *Midwest Quarterly*.

Shane Guthrie

has had his poetry alternatively called devastating, humorous, radioactive, and amusingly domestic. Popular topics include: Dealing with Low Self-Esteem, amusing anecdotes about childhood, why love is really actually pretty hard, why love is really actually pretty great.

Matthew Harrison

lives in Hong Kong, and maybe because of that his writing has veered from non-fiction to literary and he is currently reliving a boyhood passion for science fiction. He has published numerous SF short stories and is building up to longer pieces as he learns more about the universe. Matthew is married with two children but no pets. Find more of his work at www.matthewharrison.hk.

Kyle Hemmings

is a retired health care worker. He has been published in *[b]oink*, *Otata*, *Is/Let*, *Haibun Today*, *Sonic Boom*, *New World Writing*, and elsewhere. His latest collection of prose is *Split Brain* on Amazon Kindle. Kyle loves drawing, street photography, and 60s garage bands who never made mainstream.

John Herold

lives in Duluth, Minnesota. Having taught English in a rural K-12 public school, he now teaches composition to college freshmen. He loves the hiking in northeastern Minnesota, and he is not encouraging people to move into the area.

Mark Hudson

gets his poetry published in poetry anthologies, and is a never-ending art student. Lately, with the freezing cold of winter bumming him out, he was grateful to receive in the mail five anthologies of poetry which he had a piece in. He was also grateful to find out yesterday at his school holiday art show he sold two art pieces he made, which will bring him some money in the new year. He's grateful to all the editors who work so hard on these books, because he's starting to realize how much work goes into these books, and Mark is grateful to get his voice out there.

Scott Hughes

has had fiction, poetry, and essays appear in *Crazyhorse, One Sentence Poems, Entropy, Deep Magic, Carbon Culture Review, Redivider, PopMatters, Strange Horizons, Odd Tales of Wonder, The Haunted Traveler,* and *Compaso: Journal of Comparative Research in Anthropology and Sociology.* For further information, visit writescott.com.

Joanne Jagoda

retired in 2009, and one inspiring writing workshop later launched her on an unexpected writing trajectory. Her short stories, poetry and creative nonfiction appear online and in print anthologies including *Gemini, Pure Slush,* and *Better After 50.* Her poem, *Mr. Avocado Man,* was nominated for a Pushcart Prize. Joanne continues taking Bay Area writing workshops, enjoys Zumba, traveling and spoiling her seven grandchildren, who call her 'Savta'.

Susan Doble Kaluza

has work published or forthcoming from New Rivers Press' *Visiting Bob* anthology, *Tammy Journal*, *Rattle*, *Pure Slush*, *Lost River Review*, *Kentucky Review*, among others. She currently has two poetry chapbooks knocking on doors. She is a competitive runner and two-time women's national masters champion in summer biathlon. She lives with her husband in the mining town of Butte, Montana, USA, where she passionately practices the 3 Rs: Running, Writing, and Rescuing horses.

Jill Kiesow

writes fiction and poetry, and has pieces in *The Matador Review*, *Ariel Chart*, *Tuck Magazine*, and *Lunch Ticket*. She is a long-time vegan and animal advocate, has worked at a shelter, and currently volunteers for a dog rescue. She and her husband, precocious toddler, rescued cats, and adopted shelter dogs live in rural Wisconsin. Find more at www.jillkiesow.com.

Linda Kohler

is a writer from Adelaide, Australia. Her work has been published in various journals, magazines and collections, and in a poetry anthology by Wakefield Press. Linda has been a highly commended applicant for the Australian Society of Authors Poetry Mentorship program, a waitress, television scriptwriter, proofreader and teacher. She likes the natural world and it tends to appear in her stories.

Em König

is a queer poet/DJ/Winter Witch from Adelaide. Their work has featured in *On Dit*, *Flazeda*, *Uneven Floor*, et. al. They have participated in spoken word events as part of Feast Festival and in 2016 contributed work to the 'Queering The Museum' event at the South Australian Migration Museum. They were recently awarded the 2016 John Harvey Finlayson Prize for creative writing and the 2016 Sir Archibald Strong Memorial Prize for literature. Em is currently working on the collaborative music/performance/writing project *Climate of Cruelty* (www.climateofcruelty.com), which explores the links between the factory farming industry and the destruction of the environment.

Len Kuntz

is a writer from Washington State and an editor at the online magazine *Literary Orphans*. His latest story collection, *At the Deep End*, is forthcoming from Ravenna Press in June of 2018. You can also find him at lenkuntz.blogspot.com.

Bridget Kursheed

is an Australian poet and geek now based in the Scottish Borders. She is a Scottish Book Trust New Writers Award recipient for poetry, and her work is widely published in magazines including *The Rialto*, *Butcher's Dog*, *New Writing Scotland*, *Ambit*, *Zoomorphic*, and *Gutter*. In her spare time she works in software in Edinburgh and is studying for an MSc in cybersecurity. Find more @khursheb.

John Lambremont, Sr.

is a poet and writer from Baton Rouge, Louisiana, U.S.A. His poems have been published internationally in many reviews and anthologies, including *Pacific Review*, *The Minetta Review*, *Clarion*, *Flint Hills Review*, and *Taj Mahal Review*, and he has been nominated for The Pushcart Prize. John's new poetry volume is *The Moment of Capture*, Lit Fest Press (2017). John's previous poetry volumes include *Dispelling The Indigo Dream* (Local Gems Poetry Press, 2013), and a chapbook, *What It Means To Be A Man (And Other Poems Of Life And Death)* (Finishing Line Press, 2014).

Cynthia Leslie-Bole

is a writing coach, editor and certified Amherst Writers and Artists Method group leader who has been published in *Pure Slush*, *Rootstalk* and *Moonshine Ink's Creative Brew*. Her collection of poetry, *The Luminous In-Between* (Azalea Arts Press, 2016), celebrates our innate capacity to create, heal, and perceive what lies beyond the ordinary. Cynthia lives in the San Francisco Bay Area. Find more at www.cynthialesliebole.com and www.theluminousinbetween.blogspot.com.

DS Levy

has been published in *Little Fiction*, the *Alaska Quarterly Review*, *Columbia*, *South Dakota Review*, *Brevity*, and *The Pinch*, and new work will soon appear in *Door Is a Jar Magazine*, *Fictive Dream*, and *Flash: The International Short-Short Story Magazine*. Her collection of flash fiction, *A Binary Heart*, was published in 2017 by Finishing Line Press. Find her on Twitter @122cats and more of her work at deblevy1.wix.com/debraslevy.

Peter Lingard

told his mother many fantastic tales of intrepid adventures enjoyed by him and his friends when he was a youngster. She always said, "Go tell it to the Marines." When he asked why, she said, "They've been everywhere and done everything, so they'll want to hear about what you've been up to." Of course, Peter joined the Royal Marines as soon as he was old enough. He later worked as an accountant and a farm hand. Peter lived in the US for twenty-five years and owned a freight forwarding business in New York. Look for further books about Paul and Jack to be published in the future. His latest novel, *Boswell's Fairies*, is available in many stores, online, and at his website peterlingard.com.

JP Lundstrom

spent the first thirty years of her life in southern California, the locale in which her stories are often set. She writes poetry as an exercise in self-discipline, since it requires care in selecting words for meaning, meter and mood. Her books are available in e-format. Upcoming: *The Calendar Girls*, a collection of short stories and poems.

Kate Mahony

has an MA in Creative Writing from the International Institute of Modern Letters, Victoria University, New Zealand. Her fiction has been published in numerous international literary journals and print anthologies including: *The Best New Zealand Fiction #6* (Random House, New Zealand), *Landmarks* (UK, 2015), *The Fish Anthology* (Ireland, 2015), as well as in the forthcoming *Bonsai: the big book of short fiction* (Canterbury University Press, 2018). Visit www.katemahonywriter.com.

Leigh Marques

is a queer poet currently living in Philadelphia. A recent graduate of Virginia Tech, Leigh spends most of their time thinking about angels and talking about love on Twitter

@mo0ndrool. Their work can be found either published or forthcoming in *Hematopoiesis Press*, *Vagabond City Lit*, *And So Yeah Mag*, and elsewhere.

Thomas M. McDade

is a former programmer / analyst residing in Fredericksburg, VA, previously CT & RI. He is a graduate of Fairfield University, Fairfield, CT. McDade is twice a U.S. Navy Veteran serving ashore at the Fleet Anti-Air Warfare Training Center, Virginia Beach, VA, at sea aboard the USS Mullinnix (DD-944) and USS Miller (DE/FF 1091).

Kindra McDonald

received her MFA from Queens University of Charlotte. She teaches poetry at The Muse Writers Center and is an adjunct writing professor and doctoral student. She is the author of *Concealed Weapons* published by ELJ and *Elements and Briars* published by Red Bird Chapbooks. She lives in Norfolk, VA with her husband and cats and she changes hobbies monthly.

L. Noelle McLaughlin

is a ghostwriter and fiction editor. Her fiction and poetry have been featured in *The Stone Canoe Journal*, *Thrice Fiction*, *New Dead Families*, *GAMBA zine*, *Sein und Werden*, *Danse Macabre*, *Lime Hawk Literary Arts Collective*, *nth position*, *Unlikely Stories*, *Haggard and Halloo*, *Clockwise Cat*, *Sammy and Beckett*, *The Screech Owl* and more. She takes little notes on her favorite reads at poorhumanbeans.wordpress.com, and tweets @lnoellemcl.

Catherine McLeod

is a student who lives in Melbourne, Australia. Her work has appeared or is scheduled to appear in *RMIT Catalyst* and *Demos*. She hopes that her dog is happier than the one in the story published here.

Gwendolyn Joyce Mintz

is an award-winning writer. Her work has appeared in various journals and over forty anthologies. She is the author of two fiction chapbooks, *Mother Love* and *Where I'll Be If I'm Not There*.

Piet Nieuwland

is a performance poet and his poems appear in many places including *Landfall, Brief,* and *Catalyst* in New Zealand; *Mattoid, Otoliths* and *Cordite* in Australia; and *Blue Fifth Review, Lunch Ticket, Mojave River Review* and *Atlanta Review* in USA. He edits *Fast Fibres Poetry*, review's poetry for *Landfall Review Online* and lives near Whangarei. He also works on conservation strategies for Te Papa Atawhai in New Zealand.

Brian Obiri-Asare

is of Ghanaian heritage, and currently lives, breathes, works and sleeps in Sydney.

Sunayna Pal

was born and raised in Mumbai, and moved to the US after her marriage. She opted out of her corporate job to embark on her heart's pursuits – sold art for NGOs and became a certified handwriting analyst to help people understand themselves. Now, a new mother, she devotes her free time to writing and

Heartfulness (http://en.heartfulness.org). She is part of an anthology that will break the Guinness Records. Know more at sunaynapal.com.

Carl 'Papa' Palmer

of Old Mill Road in Ridgeway, VA now lives in University Place, WA. He is retired military, retired FAA and now just plain retired without wristwatch, alarm clock or Facebook friend. Carl, hospice volunteer and president of The Tacoma Writers Club, is a Pushcart Prize and Micro Award nominee. His motto: Long Weekends Forever. (Google 'Carl Papa Palmer' to read more stories of poetry and prose.)

Tim Philippart

sold his business in 2015. Since May of 2015, he has written several poems and others are scattered around his house, dropped like dirty socks. He writes, mainly, poetry and short prose pieces with, in some cases, a hint of humor.

Martin Jon Porter

is a teacher who lives in Melbourne. His most recent poetry has featured in *Short and Twisted*, *Verandah* and *Truth Serum*. His debut chapbook, *Traits*, was published by Ginninderra Press in 2016 as part of its Picaro Poets series.

Prospero Pulma Jr.

owes the editorial staff of *Alfie Dog Fiction*, *Bewildering Stories*, *Every Day Fiction*, *Every Day Poets*, *FewerThan500*, *Flash Fiction Magazine*, *Flashes in the Dark*, *Pure Slush*, *Short-Story.me*, *Short-story.net*, *Sirens Call*, *Splickety Magazine*, *The Corner Club Press*, *The Gambler Mag*, and major publications and anthologies in the Philippines a million thanks for publishing his work. You can find more at https://prosperopulma.blogspot.com/ and also at https://pepulma.wordpress.com. Soli deo Gloria!

Melisa Quigley

lives in Melbourne, Victoria, Australia with her husband and two dogs. She is a writer and poet who has had her poetry, short stories and flash fiction published in several anthologies in the US and Australia. You can find examples of her work at her website here: https://melisaquigley.wordpress.com. When she is not writing she likes reading and cooking as well as yoga.

Edward Reilly

was born in Adelaide and received his PhD in Poetics in 2000. He has been active in Geelong as a teacher and cultural organizer for the past 35 years, and now enjoys reading as widely as possible, travelling and his family. His student study guides, a travelogue, criticism and poetry have all been published.

Alex Robertson

spent his formative years in Adelaide, South Australia and occupied his early working life around (country) SA and the Northern Territory. He has been published in university newspapers and in print and online journals. Since moving to Gawler, he has been involved in writing groups and broadcasting organisations and is working on his first poetry collection.

Ruth Sabath Rosenthal

is well-published in the U.S. and also internationally. In October 2006, her poem *on yet another birthday* was nominated for a Pushcart Prize. Ruth's books – *Facing Home* (a chapbook), and four full-length books: *Facing Home & beyond*; *little, but by no means small*; *Food: Nature vs Nurture*; and *Gone, but Not Easily Forgotten* – are available from Amazon.com. Check out Ruth's websites at http://poetrybyruthsabathrosenthal.com, http://bigapplepoet.com and http://newyorkcitypoet.com.

KR Rosman

is an educator in Seattle. Her stories have appeared in *Superstition Review*, *Foxing Quarterly*, *Adirondack Review*, *Raven Chronicles*, and others.

Wayne Scheer

has been nominated for the Pushcart Prize four times, and a Best of the Net. He's had numerous stories, poems and essays published in print and online. Find *Revealing Moments*, his collection of flash stories at https://issuu.com/pearnoir/docs/revealing_momentsa. His short story, *Zen and the Art of House Painting*, has been made into a short film, which can be found at https://vimeo.com/18491827.

Robert Scotellaro

has been published in W.W. Norton's *Flash Fiction International*, *The Best Small Fictions 2016* and *2017*, and many other venues. He is the author of seven literary chapbooks and three story collections: *Measuring the Distance*, *What We Know So Far*, and *Bad Motel*. With James Thomas, he's co-edited an anthology of microfiction, due out by W.W. Norton in 2018. Robert lives in San Francisco. He can be reached at: www.rsflashfiction.com.

Margarita Serafimova

was shortlisted for the Montreal International Poetry Prize 2017. She has two collections in Bulgarian (2016 and 2017). Her work appears in *London Grip New Poetry, Trafika Europe, The Journal, A-Minor, Waxwing, StepAway, Ink, Sweat and Tears, Minor Literatures, Writing Disorder, The Birds We Piled Loosely, Noble/Gas, Obra/Artifact, Poetic Diversity, Harbinger Asylum, Ginosko, Peacock Journal, Anti-Heroin Chic,* and many other places. Find more at https://www.facebook.com/MargaritaISerafimova/.

Lisa Stice

is a poet/mother/military spouse, the author of a poetry collection *Uniform* (Aldrich Press, 2016), and a Pushcart Prize nominee. She volunteers as a mentor with the Veterans Writing Project, as an associate poetry editor with *1932 Quarterly,* and as a contributor for *The Military Spouse Book Review.* She currently lives in North Carolina with her husband, daughter and dog. You can learn more about her publications at her website https://lisastice.wordpress.com/.

E. M. Stormo

is an editor by day, writer by night, and a teacher and promoter of musical literacy at all times. His recent work has appeared in *The Conium Review, Thrice Magazine,* and *Entropy Magazine.*

Lucy Tyrrell

moved from Alaska to Bayfield, Wisconsin in November 2016, trading a big mountain (Denali) for a big lake (Superior). She holds a Ph.D. in botany from the University of Wisconsin Madison. Her favorite verbs to live by near Bayfield and Lake Superior are: *experience* (nature, outdoor adventures like mushing with her seven Alaska huskies and canoeing) and *create* (write, quilt, sketch).

Hannah van Didden

plays with words in the second most isolated capital city in the world. You will find pieces of her in places like *Hippocampus*, *Breach*, *Atticus Review*, *Southword Journal*, and at her website http://37thirtyseven.wordpress.com.

Rob Walker

lives in the nondescript suburbs of Adelaide, South Australia. He has six books of poetry, most recently *tropeland* (Five Islands Press), *Policies & Procedures* (Garron Publishing) and *original clichés* (Ginninderra Press.) He hopes to produce a collection of short stories before he dies. Find more at www.robwalkerpoet.com.

Mbeke Waseme

is a storyteller, blogger, photographer and political analyst. Her stories come from her amazing experiences as an international Educationalist and Coach Trainer who has worked within and across schools, colleges and higher education providers in the UK, Malaysia, Jamaica and Ghana. As a published poet, inspirational speaker and blogger, she values the power and vision that the spoken and written word hold. Her podcasts will further inspire those who have enjoyed her written stories and travel blogs. Find more here at: http://www.mbekewaseme.com/.

Michael Webb

is proud to be published in a number of *Pure Slush* titles while he sells drugs outside Philadelphia, Pennsylvania.

Allan J. Wills

remembers walking an alpine meadow in Kashmir thirty years ago and finding a cluster of wild strawberries that had been mislaid by another traveller. Happiness in any circumstance is such a windfall: unexpected, overwhelming and unforgettable.

Also from Pure Slush Books

http://pureslush.webs.com/store.htm

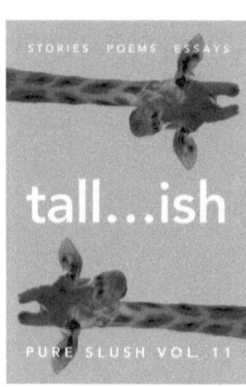

• Inane Pure Slush Vol. 14
ISBN: 978-1-925536-17-1 (paperback) / 978-1-925536-18-8 (eBook)
• Freak Pure Slush Vol. 13
ISBN: 978-1-925536-15-7 (paperback) / 978-1-925536-16-4 (eBook)
• Summer Pure Slush Vol. 12
ISBN: 978-1-925536-13-3 (paperback) / 978-1-925536-14-0 (eBook)
• tall…ish Pure Slush Vol. 11
ISBN: 978-1-925101-80-5 (paperback) / 978-1-925101-98-0 (eBook)
• Five Pure Slush Vol. 10
ISBN: 978-1-925101-71-3 (paperback) / 978-1-925101-72-0 (eBook)
• Feast! Pure Slush Vol. 9
ISBN: 978-1-925101-62-1 (paperback) / 978-1-925101-63-8 (eBook)